Once Upon @ Dream Or Two

By Isabel K. T.

Doodles By Isabel K. T.

Illustrations By Nicorene Stassen

1...2...3...

First published in the United States of America on 2023 by Calelei™ Productions.

If you would like to use any material from this book please contact us at
hello@caleleiproductions.com

ISBN: 978-1-958807-12-5
Color ISBN: 978-1-958807-40-8
eISBN: 978-1-7363180-0-3

Library of Congress Control Number: 2022921762

ABOUT THIS BOOK:
"Once Upon A Dream Or Two " By Isabel K.T.
First Edition, July 2023   I   First Print, July 2023   I   English Language
Second Edition, June 2024   I   Second Print, June 2024   I   English Language
The fonts used in this book were "Dawning of a New Day" for the cover, "Quicksand" for the chapter headings, "Bellota" for details, and "Open Sans" for the story and all other text. Cover art by Nicorene Stassen. Cover design by Isabel K.T. and Nicorene Stassen. Illustrations by Nicorene Stassen. Doodles by Isabel K.T.

Please note that the publisher is not responsible for any other website (or content) other than the publishers'. Visit us anytime:

Calelei™ Productions
www.caleleiproductions.com

We love Trees. Follow our tree planting at caleleiproductions.com/trees

"TO THE MAN OF MY DREAMS — I LOVE YOU"

"When most I wink then do mine eyes best see

For all the day the view things unrespected;

But when I sleep, in dreams I look on thee

And darkly bright are bright and dark directed.

Then thou whose shadow shadows doth make

bright,

How would thy shadow's form form happy show

To the clear day with thy much clearer light

When to unseeing eyes thy shade shines so!

How would, I say, mine eyes be blessed made

By looking on thee in the living day

When in dead night thy fair imperfect shade,

Through heavy sleep on sightless eyes doth stay

All days are night to see till I see thee,

And nights bright days when dreams do show

thee me. "

- William Shakespeare, Sonnet 43

[Star-Kissed]

I've heard it said that we are all made up of star-dust. I have also heard it said that there are moments so precious that the stars must have aligned for them to happen. Could it be then that it is not the stars above that align for us, rather that we — as star-dust — align within ourselves, and in so doing we align with the stars above in a glorious movement of harmony and bliss... Perhaps it is in this alignment that we too align with the particular star-dust we share most closely on earth... Perhaps it is because of this movement that everything falls into place for serendipity to happen... Perhaps it is in this harmony that love shines so bright it reaches beyond time and space to bring two hearts together... Perhaps ...

1.2.3.4...

WINTER

1..2..3...

The place is deserted. Long spaces of green gently blown by a cool breeze set the stage. Three people appear on scene. Friends. They laugh jokingly as they look around for a place to sit. The entirety of the fields before them is a viable option. The music hasn't started, yet the lineup promises a busy and entertaining day ahead. One of the boys in the group sees a familiar face and waves in welcome. She turns to see who it is.

He walks up in a long coat with a bright smile and embraces his friend in the unmistakable form of a warm hug. As he turns to introduce himself to her, their eyes meet. A sudden realization hits: he can see her. She catches her breath, freezing on the spot. Not the ice kind of freeze where your veins feel the sudden jolt of time slowing down. The magnetic kind. The kind that awakens every ounce of you and starts moving every particle, ever so gently, in the same direction. A sense of alertness and harmony follows.

"Hello," he says with a smile as he stretches out his hand to meet hers.
She feels her hand begin to move in his direction. His voice sounds reassuringly familiar, and just like

that — in one soft movement — her world begins

to change...

SPRING

It's late. The light outside looks like midnight but the air boasts of early morning. As she walks in she notices people leaving. The bright remains of a party lay splattered across the floor and furniture. He sits at the bar. She knows he's been waiting. The thought cements her to the spot if only for a moment. Her heart rate inches towards running away. She takes a deep breath and makes a decision.

"Hello," she says as she reaches his side.

He turns ever so slightly to see her slowly sitting down next to him. He smiles brightly in welcome, "Hello."

As his smile breaches the space between them, she feels the comfort of the reunion ease her fear away.

"Have you been waiting long?" She asks.

He answers calmly, his smile unmovable, "Yes."

"I'm sorry," she says trying to avoid his gaze, "it's taken me longer than I expected."

"It's ok. I'm not going anywhere."

His calm certainty hits a nerve in her heart and before she can think twice about it the words escape her lips, "That's what scares me."

She turns her head away; half in fear, half in embarrassment. He reaches out to touch her hand.

"You see," she continues emboldened by the kind gesture, "I feel as if I just got my heart back, and while you are not asking for it, it certainly feels like it knows where to go," she takes a deep breath, "and I know that if I start sharing it with you it will change the safety I feel now. I feel pulled to you in a way that scares me. Even my words seem to know where to go, and my voice what to say, without my intervention."

His smile widens. She can feel the warmth of his smile spreading gently on her cheeks. He says nothing. She looks up to meet his gaze.

"You are not scared?" she asks.

He pauses for a moment, a single moment of deep contemplation. "I am scared of what happens when you leave," he says gently. He tries to smile, but worry is a potent weight tugging at the corner of his lips. "When you appear, even in silence, it takes away the lonely I did not even know I was feeling."

"Are you very lonely?" She asks.

"Waiting is a lonely place," he answers candidly. His own answer seems to surprise him.

"What are you waiting for?"

"I think I have been waiting for you." He takes his hand away from hers and straightens up in his chair, distancing himself from her a little. "I did not mean to share that. I do not mean to keep you if you want to leave. It's just... I am here and I know this is where I need to be... although I am not even sure how I got here to begin with..."

She smiles at the reassurance that this encounter is a shared space of new. "I know exactly what you mean," she says.

Her hand reaches out to his. He looks up to see her smiling and feels relieved that his honesty did not scare her away. They smile at each other. The freedom of being absolutely understood engulfs them in a single moment that seems to touch forever, holding them to the spot — and to each other— by the harmony in their grins.

1..2..3...

SUMMER

"Where are we?" She looks around. Everything feels like a moving picture — static yet alive, flat yet three dimensional. A creek nearby marks time with gentle ripples on the pebbles within. At least that is a given, time does not stand still.

"I'm not sure," he says smiling, "I've lost track. Should we keep going?" He extends his hand. She takes it. They walk along an unmarked road in silent unison as luscious green foliage outlines their journey. The distinguishable height difference does not alter the sync in their steps. Each step is taken naturally, each foot at its own pace, yet completely comfortable — at home — in the shared rhythm.

After a moment she stops and letting go of his hand she gently tugs on his arm in a silent request to face each other. He follows her suggested movement. She looks at his face searching for something along the gentle fine lines that define his features.

"Can I help you?" He asks.

"I am trying to find you in my memory. How do I know you? I feel like we have met before. Long ago perhaps?"

"Please do, I cannot find you in mine. I've looked. Your face is engraved in my every thought."

She smiles. "Ditto," she says matter-of-factly.

"Ditto… hmm… ditto seems too small a word," he says.

"I can't seem to find a better one. My sentiments echo yours and it feels like *ditto* — a short and fleeting sound capsule that can hold an un-containable world of depth and meaning."

"Is that where we are? In a world of depth and meaning?" he asks.

"Or something in between," she blushes.

"If I'm honest, I don't care about the where, just that you are in it." He reaches for her hand and tenderly finds her fingers.

The crimson of her cheeks subsides into a smile. "You always know how to make things comfortable," she says.

"I thought you were the one doing that," he answers. He looks at the grass around them, the space has opened up. The trees that seconds ago delineated their walk now form the outside perimeter on a wide meadow. The brushstrokes on the grass look like they've known time since it's beginning while the freshness in the air paints the space in joyous welcome. She looks around at the grass hoping to understand what he is seeing.

"What are we looking for?" She asks.

"Flowers. I am looking for flowers," he smiles, "I wanted to bring you flowers, but I wasn't sure. I thought you might like flowers. Do you?"

Touched by the gesture she just nods and smiles back, "I do like flowers."

"What kind of flowers do you like?"

"Possibly all of them. There are a few at the top of my list though there seem to be flowers for me to love on all occasions. Wild bright pink roses are a particular favorite. I am not sure they are actually wild or called wild for that matter they just have a free look about them, the petals seem to flow multidimensionally as if they grew in dance to their own rhythm... I like planting them best though, with a little love and care you can watch them bloom over and over again... So yes, I love flowers, specially colorful ones."

"We'll that's good. I am sure I will be able to find flowers plural somewhere around here."

"It's ok, the thought counts you know?" she reaches four his hand and intertwines her fingers along his.

The air around them breaths and in a sudden movement a gentle breeze brings them closer together. The space that surrounds them blooms as flowers of all colors appear outlining the intimacy of a newly birthed meadow. There are daffodils, camellias, peonies, daisies, tulips, sunflowers, orchids, and yes — wild roses. Something falls on her shoulder, she looks up. The trees have bloomed too and jacaranda petals in kindred shades of lavender and blue softly fall towards them cascading the space with snowlike wonder.

"When did this happen?" She asks surprised.

"I think... while we were speaking, or perhaps as we spoke..." he looks at the horizon before returning his gaze to her. For the first time there is sadness in his eyes. "We have wondered off. It's almost morning."

He bends down to pick a flower close to them, her hand quickly rests upon his gently stopping his action. She bends down towards the flowers by his hand and takes in the lovely smell, leaving them where they are.

"Thank you for my flowers. They smell lovely." She gives him a soft kiss on the cheek.

"I am glad you liked them. I put in a good word," he smiles blushing a little.

She matches his smile, "It shows! And what a perfect arrangement."

She takes a step back to frame the flowers and shrubs between her fingers, "Truly a work of art and exactly how I would have placed them." She laughs in delight. Her laugh echos through space in a stream of chimes and bubbles that knows no bounds. He closes his eyes and lets the melody run through him in a hum.

"Come on," she says, "Let's enjoy what's left of our walk before sunrise catches up with us." He opens his eyes. Her hand is extended before him. He takes it. They walk into what is left of the night. The soft tendrils of dawn mark each step. A gust of wind picks up the fallen flower petals from the ground and swirls them around in a colorful palette of periwinkles as everything transitions into morning.

FALL

She walks into the night. Fireflies fly above. They sprinkle the air with supple light as a blanket of stars covers the indigo depths of a cool night. A path has been illuminated for her and he stands at the end of it. A picnic blanket lays on the grass next to him.

"You found me," he smiles as he extends his hand.

She takes it and joins him on the blanket, "I did. What's all this?"

"I thought we could look at the stars and enjoy the night."

"I like it," she lays down. He quickly lays next to her.

They look on at the night sky in silence. A whisper reaches her ear. *"Dum da di di di di dum da di di di di di da..."*

"What's that?" She asks.

"Hmm? What's what?"

"The melody."

"Oh, it's something I've been working on," he answers blushing a little.

"Oh," she says intrigued "How does it go?"

"That's as far as I've gotten. Do you like it?"

"I do," she looks at the stars, "It's the perfect soundtrack for a night like this." She sighs and reaches out to hold his hand, "The stars are so vibrant. It's almost like they are dancing."

"Do you see that one there?" He points straight above their heads.

"The bright yellowish one?" She asks.

"Yes. Do you know what it is?" He asks.

"I have absolutely no clue," she turns to face him, "Do you?"

He smiles his cheeky smile, "Not a one. I was hoping you did."

They laugh. That is all they need to do when they are together, smile and laugh and it's enough to light up an entire life in-between meetings.

"I do know what that one is though," he points towards a bright moving point in the horizon.

"A shooting star!" She sits up excited, "Quick make a wish!"

She closes her eyes before he can say a word and wishes with all her heart for this to last forever. He just looks on at her and smiles. When she opens her eyes she finds he is doing the same. What he is wishing for she doesn't know, yet the way the lines on his face concentrate on his closed-eyed expression tell of a deep wish being made. He feels her gaze and slowly opens his eyes.

"I didn't mean to interrupt," she says.

"It's alright," he smiles.

"Did you make a wish?" She asks.

"I did, though darling, I am pretty sure that was a plane," he says gently.

"A plane?" She asks surprised, "What would a plane be doing here?"

"Well they fly people across—"

"Very funny, that's not what I meant. I am pretty sure that was a star." She looks up to the place where she saw the star just seconds before, "See, it's gone. A plane takes longer to cross the night sky."

"Yes, though a shooting star moves faster than our little shining friend."

"What would an airplane be doing here?" She asks again.

"I have no idea. What would a shooting star?" He says.

"It's more magical. Besides, I would never have an airplane in a dream," she clarifies.

"So this is a dream then?" He asks.

"Isn't it?" She answers hopeful.

"It is definitely *my* dream," he says certain.

"You are mistaken. It is *mine*. It has to be." Her words and her tone start to reveal the little clouds of doubt that accompany her mornings.

"Yet you would never have an airplane in a dream," he answers assuredly.

"Not crossing the night sky in a moment like this no. That's why it had to be a shooting star," she explains matter-of-factly.

"Why?" He turns to look at her, curious to find out what she will say next.

"Have you ever seen the bloopers to a film where mid-scene an airplane flies over and completely breaks the illusion? If they are not meant to be there, airplanes take you out of the narrative completely, and I like being immersed in a story. More so if it's my own." She lays her head back on the blanket and returns her eyes upward, "So yes, my dream wouldn't do that."

"Well that must prove it then, this isn't *your* dream," he answers confidently.

She laughs, "I wish I could tell this wasn't *my* dream."

"Oh, I am sure of it," he answers.

"Really?" She asks hopeful.

"Yes, it's mine." The smile on his face expands with assurance.

"But I know I am real, and when I wake up I remember all of this, always," she says certain.

"I do too," he answers echoing the same certainty.

"Hmm..." she thinks on.

"Hmm..." he matches, waiting for her next thought.

"Ok, let's try this," she says assuredly, "If this is my dream then we will now be floating on a cloud."

Nothing happens. He holds back a laugh.

"Ok, now you give it a try," she says.

"Ok, if this is my dream then stars will fall down from the sky as edible — mini of course — gummies," he puts out his hands.

"Were you a Wonka fan as a kid?" She asks.

"The candy forest was my favorite scene." They wait for a second more. Nothing happens.

"Now what?" He asks.

She sighs, "Perhaps this is the future. A premonition of what's to come?" She suggests.

"Based on the past? A distant memory?" He offers.

"I think if you were in my past I would definitely remember you," she says.

"We must have crossed each other at some point. If this is real—"
She raises a quizzical looking eyebrow at him.

He continues, "just indulge me for a moment, if this is real, how is it we found each other?"

"Hmm... well, how is it anyone finds each other? Is it really so very different from finding someone among the billions of people on earth?" She says, knowing she is partly explaining it to herself as she speaks.

"Fair," he readily answers, silently hoping this logic is enough to make things real.

"Maybe we are both too distracted to find each other in real life and our subconsciouses had to intervene. Maybe we cross each other all the time and we don't even know it!" She suggests.

"Maybe. It could be," he smiles thinking at the possibility, "If that is the case then I am glad they did."
She is silent.

He clarifies further, "Our subconsciouses intervening that is."

"Oh, I know what you mean," she smiles, "I was just thinking... What if we leave each other breadcrumbs? A little trail of clues to find each other?"

"Alright, what kind?"

"Any kind. Things only we would know about. Although..." she sits up and looks at him steadily, her mind made up.

"What is it?"

"May I try something — that is, I'd like to try something..." she looks a little worried.

"What would you like to try?"

She leans in, "May I kiss you?"

"Please."

She moves forward, he stays unmovable — hoping not to scare her away. Lips connect and senses relax to the soft feathery touch of warmth as bliss takes over. There is no movement, no further action, just the gentle synergy between two hearts expressed in reverence by lips. She moves back and they look at each other in silence.

"Well, if that's not real, I don't know what is," he says.

She looks at him in awe as her hand reaches for her own lips; partly to verify they are still there, partly to touch by extension the magic of the moment passed.

She lets her thoughts out in a whisper, "How can this be?"

"I don't know," He leans closer to touch her cheek, "I just know I don't want this to end. Is that alright?"

She looks at him — his eyes are full of hope and tenderness — and her heart lightens. She nods and reaches for his hand, placing hers over his, keeping his on her cheek for as long as possible.

WINTER

1..2..3...

She looks at her phone for the time. It is barely dawn. The sun will start showing against the glass walls of her room at any moment now. She looks around a bit bewildered, certain it was all just a dream again. Everything felt like a dream, but he, he never does. There he was again, just as real as her, laughing with her. *What did they talk about? Were they talking about Christmas music and holiday plans? Was there a discussion over the proper way to make sangria?* She can't quite remember this time.

The gentle streams of first light start pouring into her bedroom and with full consciousness of what needs to get done in the day ahead she decides to wake up. She hops out of bed, turns on her speakers to a peppy and energetic morning playlist — her wake up songs *du moment* — and proceeds to get ready for the day ahead...

Dionne Warwick's "I say a little prayer for you" starts playing in the background as she brushes her teeth. *If you were real, and I really (really) hope that you are, I would be saying one for you too* she thinks... She sighs and selects the song to post onto her IM-LISTENING account.

"You have been very quiet lately," D draws her attention back to the little cafe they have been sitting at for the last half hour.

"Have I?" She answers half-knowing her sister speaks the truth.

"Uncharacteristically so," reiterates D.

"I was daydreaming."

"You've been doing a lot of that too."

She sighs, "I can't help it. My dreams have been so wonderful lately it's been hard not to. I keep hoping I can pick up right where I left off."

"That's nice. I haven't had a dream I remember in ages."

"So how was your audition? I'm sorry, I totally spaced out."

"I noticed. It was good, it felt good. You know how it is, I'll have to wait to really find out. So, in the meantime, I have decided to feel good about it and just see where it leads me."

"That's nice," she answers.

"What's up?" D asks suspiciously.

"What do you mean?" She grabs the single page long menu laying untouched on the table in front of her and starts to peruse the items on it.

"You are usually more generous with your words. A lot more generous."

"It's been an odd day..." She discontinues that train of thought by asking, "At what time did we say we'd meet the girls again?"

"6:30."

"Oh, great. I have time to get something then."

"A few minutes. What kind of odd?" asks D hoping to continue that conversation.

"Good odd," she answers.

"Am I getting details?"

"As soon as I order," she sets the menu down on the table, "although, full disclosure, I am still figuring out some details myself and it may not be half as interesting as you have already imagined."

"Fair. Go order then, my curiosity is growing," says D.

She gets up to order, "Patience is a virtue…"

"Not my favorite one."

Her trip to the counter lasts about two minutes due to the lack of a line and the amount of workers present at that time of day. She returns with a to-go cup holding her almond milk matcha latte and a craft bag hosting a French viennoiserie.

"We'll be eating dinner in less than half an hour," chimes D.

"Live a little," she grabs a piece of the pain-au-chocolat from the bag and places the bag in front of D, "so it all starts sometime between when I go to bed and dawn."

"So while you sleep?" Asks D sneaking a slight peek at the pain-au-chocolat in front of her, "Is this about a dream?"

"Dreams plural, and that's the thing, I am dreaming and then I am not so sure I am dreaming anymore."

"Oh, so like a very vivid dream?" Asks D, "Are you dreaming of someone?"

"This is…it's something else. It's like I am dreaming *with* someone."

She proceeds to tell her sister the general story of the dreams that suddenly became a place of meeting.

"And then?" Asks D.

"And then what?" She answers.

"Well what happens after the dreams?"

"I wake up. What kind of question is that?"

"Do the dreams change you in any way?" Asks D while eyeing the pain-au-chocolat.

"I wake up more and more in love with someone I don't know is real," she says.

"I mean it's not that hard to fall in love with the literal man of your dreams," says D, giving in and finally reaching for a corner piece of the pain-au-chocolat.

"Correction, this is not the man *of* my dreams, this is the man *in* my dreams. Although, come to think of it, he might be both."

"See? Maybe it's life telling you to open your heart again, getting you excited about love."

She sighs, secretly hoping there is more to it, "Perhaps... it just feels so very real."
D pauses to think for a moment and takes a sip from her turmeric latte, "So you are saying you

were asleep in these dreams, and somehow you woke up in the dreams, and there was someone else who woke up with you there — in the dreams?"

"We didn't suddenly wake up. It's more like we walked into these particular segments of my dreams both awake. Or maybe they were segments of his dreams? Perhaps there is a dream space in between where we just meet? I am unsure at this point."

"Oh." D takes another minuscule piece of her self-designated corner of the pain-au-chocolate and proceeds to separate the chocolate from the bread before taking a bite of the chocolate alone.

"Oh?" She asks

"They were good dreams right?" Asks D.

"Uff. Always wonderful," she answers.

"Then that's great," D grabs her purse and stands up, "Come on, let's go eat. I'm starving, and I am starting to think you might need some real food in your system. Have you been eating well?"

"I am perfectly fine." She takes a gulp from her matcha latte, grabs the craft bag with what remains of the chocolatine, and follows her sister out of the cafe.

It's a quick walk across the open hallway that defines that particular avenue to get to the small sushi restaurant in front. Her phone rings when she reaches the door. She looks down at the screen just as someone opens the door for her to pass. Absentmindedly, she thanks them and holds the door with her body until she can free her hand. A familiar feeling surprises her, a sudden tingling at the back of her neck urges her to look up. She does. She looks around. She sees a tall figure turn the corner. She shakes off the feeling and walks in. The small restaurant was a serendipitous find. It is an intimate space that remains quiet, friendly, and always delicious, which makes it ideal for every kind of occasion. D is waiting at a table by a corner window, S is with her. She walks towards them.

A lovely melody catches her attention. It seems to come from a nearby table. The tune sounds familiar yet not familiar enough to shake up her recollection.

"Who sings this? It sounds familiar," she asks as she sits down.

"Right? No clue, but I don't think it's the last we'll hear of this one," says S.

"It's catchy. Shazam?" Says D without looking away from her menu.

She opens Shazam but there is too much ambiance noise around them for it to pick up the song. Her phone rings again. It is the same notification as before. She opens it to see @willandheart has started following her IM-LISTENING stream and responded to her post by tagging Madonna's "Like A Prayer." She smiles and puts her phone away.

"So how's your night looking?" She asks S.

"Finals are in. I have about 100 papers to get through, and then I am a free woman."

"Is 'enjoy' the right sentiment?" She asks.

"Sure, why not?" Says S laughing. "I'll try. To be fair, it's the number I dread. These kids really connected to the material. I'm excited to see what they came up with."

D finally puts down her menu and fully joins the previous conversation, "I like their sound."

The waiter — Marcuz not Mark as his name-tag would suggest — stops by. In one swift sentence he is sure to explain what happened with his name tag and asks them to continue to call him Marcuz in order to stay consistent with his brand. "One never knows when fate will knock on the door," he says.

"Granted one has to believe in fate to recognize it," she follows.

"Ain't that the truth! So what are we having? Omakase?" Marcuz asks.

They all answer in unison, "Yes, please."

"That's three Omakases please..."

"Actually," she faintly hears her sister say... "I think I'll add a miso cappuccino to my order." More was probably said because a green tea appeared in front of her moments later, yet she could not remember ordering it. The melody had caught her attention once more and she had tuned out as the lyrics to the song in the background became clearer to her: *"We wished upon a star... you were my dream come true... Haven't we met before? All I can see is you... We walk along the road, your laughter's in the air, and when the sun comes up I can't find you anywhere..."*

"Right?" Says D taking her away from her reverie.

"Right?" She answers completely distracted as she excitedly realizes she may have a breadcrumb to finding him after all. *Perhaps it's the season...* she thinks, *perhaps the odds are in their favor... perhaps the stars are aligned... perhaps fate just knocked... "perhaps" just became a lovely word... isn't that a song ?...*

"Wait, right to what?" She asks D realizing she just answered something and she has no clue what her sister is talking about.

S laughs, "Where are you?"

She sighs, "Somewhere over the rainbow probably."

"Most likely I'd say," says D sighing as well, "I was just saying we do want to see the Sake list."

"Oh... right," she turns to her friend. "S?"

"I'm skipping, as much as I want to, sake and me are not a good combination for grading and I want that to-do list crossed tonight."

"Or it could be the best gift your student's get this holiday season," says G.

"Or that, yes — so no."

"Grinchy," says D "I like it!"

"Alright ladies, here it is," says Marcuz bringing back the sake menu. He places a small postcard on-top showcasing a zoomed shot of a deep brown bottle with a warm cinnamon colored label and a golden tidal wave in the shape of a crescent moon. The name "Sleeping Beauty" is written in a golden brushstroke font atop it.

"Sleeping Beauty?" She asks

"Hiyaoroshi — it is basically the Sleeping Beauty sake. Every year a sake brand comes out with let's say their winter vintage. It is called Hiyaoroshi, and they translate it to Sleeping Beauty because the sake is brewed and then placed to sleep until the cold weather comes. So come autumn, Sleeping Beauty awakens."

"That sounds lovely," she says.

"Sleeping beauties have to awaken at some point right?" Says Marcuz "So can I interest you lovely ladies in a glass?"

"Hey it could be the antidote to your sleepy days," says D.

"Very funny," she says to her sister, "I will try it though."

"One Sleeping Beauty. Anyone else?"

"I'll have a glass of your plum wine please, and yes— I am fully aware it is a dessert wine."

"Okay. One Sleeping Beauty and a self-aware plum wine for D. Lovely. S?"

"Just keep filling up my matcha cup, I am pulling an all-nighter."

"Done, done, and done. See you all lovelies soon." Marcuz leaves and goes back towards the kitchen.

"So how are things with you?" She asks S.

"I was just telling D, this is it. The final batch. I have the weekend to finish grading and then my teaching days are over."

"That's so exciting!" She says.

"Are you going home for the break?" D asks.

"I leave next Thursday and come back on the 28th."

"I thought you were going to spend New Year's at home," she says.

"That was the original plan but since I was able to be home for Diwali, I can now go there for Christmas and come back here for New Year's with you guys."

"Oh, I think you did tell me this. I'm sorry I've been a bit distracted lately."

"Yep," chimes D.

"You've said," she sighs.

"What? It's true, you've been off somewhere else lately," repeats D.

"You have been a bit aloof these past few weeks, is everything alright?" S asks.

"Weeks?" Scoffs D.

"I am fine. I've been having these amazing dreams and D just thinks I may be low on nutrients."

"Hey that is just my first thought. You know how I get when I am hungry."

"Wait, G what kind of dreams? Do tell!" Says S.

"I've been having these repeatedly amazing dreams with a man I've never met," she shares.

"What kind of amazing?" asks S, clearly invested in the subject that seems to bore her sister.

"Soul to soul kind of amazing," she sighs.

"Ok, not what I was expecting, go on…" says S.

"Nothing about this is something you could expect. They are magical and wonderful, and feel completely real. There are things I know there is no way I could make up and others that come right out of my favorite stories. It's like they blur a fine line between dreams and reality."

"I will say it with love. I am concerned. You've been keeping to yourself a lot lately. Maybe that's why the line is looking fine or even blurry," suggests D.

"I see you every day," she tells her sister and then turns to S, "and I see you almost every day."

"Yes, but that's because I am family and S is practically family. When was the last time you met someone new, or more to my point went on a date?"

"What is the point? I fall asleep when I date and I date when I fall asleep. Besides I prefer the later. I love every second I am in them and they free up my day to do all the other things I want to do with my life."

"That's what worries me. It sounds like you are starting to rely on those dreams a bit too much," says D.

"It's not like that. Not really," she thinks for a moment, "Do you know the feeling you get when you try something and you love doing it and it turns out you have a talent for it? I'm not saying I have a talent for dreaming, I mean do you know that feeling of connecting? When something resonates with you so deeply that you can see yourself doing it forever... It's not that you actively chose to do it — although once you discover it you completely would — it's more like you connected with it and the connection was already there long before your discovery began. It's like that. It's like I'm suddenly recognizing something that already was, something I somehow have known all along."

"Except it is in a dream," says D pointedly.

"Except it is in a dream... I wish I could argue with that," she says, "I am fine though, I promise. You know I am not shy of asking for help if I need it."

"That is true," concedes D.

"Why don't you tell us the dreams? Maybe there is something they are trying to tell you?" Says S.

"I'm not sure I am ready to share them, they are still a bit of a wish blown on a birthday candle."

"Ummm maybe you are on a journey and it is this meeting that brings about that new stage in your life? Maybe you are on a journey to meet the love of your life and this is just an introduction? Journeys end in lover's meeting you know?" Suggests S.

"Perhaps..." she smiles at the thought and her smile widens as she recognizes her chosen word.

"Great. She won't want to wake up now!" Says D.

"I mean, who would?" Says S laughing.

She laughs too, "Right? See? S gets it."

"You know what? All of this is fine as long as you come out with me next time I go out. I want to be sure you don't get stuck living in a daydream," says D.

"Fine, as long as it is something fun," she says.

"I'm sorry I'm late. Traffic is ridiculous, they blocked half the street for a taping and I had to go all the way around," says J sitting down next to D.

"Not a problem, we are just catching up," she answers.

J grabs a menu and turns to her friends, "Did you order the usual?"

"We did and today's specials are on the back!" S answers knowingly.
J turns the menu, looks it over in a matter of seconds, nods, and places it down on the table in what could be seen as a single swift move.

"Ok, I'm set. So, what did I miss?" Says J, looking around.

"S will be here for New Year's, I am just hungry — oh and waiting to hear back from an audition— and G is having some amazing dreams

that are making it hard to wake up in the morning,"
says D pointing at her sister.

"That sounds almost like an accusation,"
she says laughing, "it's not like that. Yes, I am
having these amazing dreams, and yes I don't want
them to end, but no, I am not having trouble with
my day to day thank you very much. I thought we
covered that."

"That's not what I meant, well, not *exactly*
what I meant," says D.

"To be clear. You have been very, very,
vocal on your worry and I promise you the
message has been received," she answers smiling
at her sister.

"D thinks she may need to eat better, I
think it's a journey to love or self-discovery, what do
you think?" S asks J.

"I think dreams can be powerful. You know
my cousin started having these dreams just before
her wedding. Not those kinds of dreams just
dreams that were really rilling her up. Someone
recommended a dream specialist. Let me get you
her name."

"Thanks for the offer J, but I am not sure I want to share any of this with a professional. This town is filled with professionals for all kinds of inexplicable things and I just don't want to fall into an accidental rabbit hole or be told what this is."

"No, no, this woman is not like that. This is a trained psychologist who just also happens to be a dream guru. Trained in the orient somewhere."

"Hmm…There's a lot of ground to cover in that sentence," points out S.

"I know, I know, you know I don't mean anything by it. I fall under that umbrella too. I just have absolutely no idea where exactly. This way I am covering all my bases," says J.

"Hello babies," A — walks up to the table still finishing a text. Her left hand places a bag on the chair in front of her while the right keeps her fingers moving with alacrity. "What did I miss?"

"Dream talk," says S succinctly.

"Oooh sounds great." A's phone starts to ring. "I want to hear everything but I have to take this. They sent me the wrong fabrics. Can you order for me?"

"Sure. What do you want?" She says.

"Anything that's not too fishy. I trust your judgement," says A as she answers the phone "Alo..."

"Mom texted by the way, she says she loved the design you sent, and to give her a call back. Also, W and Dad said they sent you a sample of the fabric they are working on, they said to tell you to please look it over and see if it can now work for the racing prototype."

A nods her head and gives her a thumbs up before walking away to take the call.

"Oh she told me too," says D "I completely forgot to tell her."

"What? You forgot?" She says.

"Even perfection is human," says D with a grin, "I never said I didn't forget things."

G laughs and shakes her head.

J's phone rings with a bright holiday chime. "It's my cousin, I just forwarded you the text. You can just text the lady and tell her your dream and if you don't like the response or feel uncomfortable you don't have to go meet her beyond that."

She sighs, "Thanks. I am loving the support guys, I am, I just want to take my time with this. I promise that when I am ready to figure more of this out I will let you all know."

"Of course, you do it on your time, just know you have the resource. I just sent you the contact info," says J with a smile.

"Thanks! So about New Year's ?" She says changing the subject...

"Dum da di di di di di di...dum da di di di di..." the melody is still on her mind when she arrives home a few hours later. With all her holiday to-do list officially done, she is looking forward to falling asleep. Maybe she'll bump into a nice dream. She hopes she will. Her phone rings, she looks down and @willandheart just posted Paul McCartney's "Wonderful Christmastime" to his listening stream. She looks at his profile, a melange of melodies that span decades and genres greets her. *Hey, it's like mine* she thinks... She smiles, follows him back, and presses play on his holiday post.

As she walks into her bedroom, she immediately sees her unmade bed. *New Year's resolution number 1, always make your bed before you leave the room.* She sighs and walks over to finish. For some reason making the bed in the morning has a satisfaction to it, making it in the evening just feels like a chore yet it needs to be done. If there is something she enjoys is sleeping in nice crisp bedsheets. She yawns, *these bed thoughts are only making me more sleepy...*

The bed! That's it! It's the melody — Dum da di di di di di — it's the melody she's been humming the last few weeks when she wakes up. It wasn't just the dream lyrics she picked up at the restaurant, she knew the melody was familiar. *Could this be it? Was this really a breadcrumb?* Her heart starts pounding to a brand new rhythm. Her excitement permeates the air.

She walks over to her bookshelf. Months of research line every shelf with books and articles on dream meanings and dream theories, from quantum enigmas to folklore that spans the globe. As she absentmindedly reaches out for one of the books she bumps into the side of the shelf. The rolled yoga mat that normally stands on the bottom left shelf falls to the ground and an idea quickly forms.

"I wonder…" she sits down right where she stands, closes her eyes, and takes a deep breath…

"Hello? Are you there?" No response. Not even a visual cue to show location.

She takes a deep breath and tries again. "I am not sure if you can hear me. I was thinking… if we really are communicating in dreams, perhaps, perhaps you can hear me like this too… Perhaps… I know this sounds silly, for all I know I am just talking to myself… Would this be considered talking to myself? I don't know…" She shakes her head and returns to the original train of thought. "Ok, I thought of something… I need a sign, something clear that can't be misconstrued. Something that shows me you are living this too. I need to know this is not just me or my imagination giving me a new avenue to process love. I'll never know if I don't try right?"

She takes a deeper breath. "I'm here. I am listening. I just need a sign from your end. Show me this is a two-way street and I will find a way to answer back… I was thinking… I had an idea… if you can hear me… I think I've found out a way to know who you are… I think I heard your song… what if when you make a video to that song… to ensure it is a sign and *not just a plausible misunderstanding... How about, in your video, you show me you are looking for me? Or looking for someone? Let that be the message... Do anything that shows me you are searching... That you are looking for a way back... Run, swim, drive, sail, fly, anything that shows me you are in pursuit... I will keep an eye out and if you send this signal I will find a way to answer. I'll know this is real and I will find a way to meet you half way. I promise..."* She slowly opens her eyes and hopes with all her heart that her words find their intended destination.

Once that is said, once that is done, she makes a conscious choice to return to her life with an open heart — leaving everything else to be — while the hope for possibility effervescently sprinkles her mind.

SPRING

She wakes up with the unmistakable feeling of jocose laughter coursing through her body. He must have been there again. She only laughs like that with him. She tries to remember. *She wore an itsy, bitsy, teenie, weenie, yellow, polka dot bikini...* starts playing on repeat in her head. *Is that it?* A sudden craving for grapefruit juice directs her thoughts towards the kitchen. *The kitchen.* There was a kitchen... *Were they cooking something on a stove top and debating about what to sweeten it with? Honey? Agave? Maple syrup? Coconut sugar? Cajeta? What was it? Nutella? It had to have been something sweet.* There was a faint memory of sweetness. It was a breakfast for dinner kind of thing. *Was this one real or just the remnants of wishful thinking?* It had been months since she could remember a dream. Only bits and pieces stayed with her when she woke up.

There was a game of Candyland, one of Clue, a conversation about solving mysteries and Scooby-Doo, a long drive to the beach, watching the sunrise by the sea shore, filming with a 16mm camera — she only knew it was a 16mm camera because she distinctly remembers snippets of a conversation in which she made a point four the camara selection as part of the storytelling process — swimming, popcorn and movies on a couch, cozy naps, long walks, bonfires, a party, roller-blading, sharing ice cream with chocolate flavored rainbow colored sprinkles, conversations over tea or was it coffee? Segments, that's all she had. Segments that seemed barely beyond reach, as if they were on the other side of a thin—albeit currently foggy—crystal.

She could see the moments showcased yet they stayed just far enough away for her to tell what they were. She sighs, presses play on her playlist, and turns on her speakers to find the last verses of Bryan Hyland's "Itsy Bitsy Tiny Weenie, Yellow Polka Dot Bikini" playing. *What was that?* She jumps out of bed as she grabs her phone, her IM-LISTENING app is still synched to her playlists and @willandheart had posted this song moments earlier. She likes the post and adds the song to her playlist. She sighs... *if only finding him were that easy... perhaps she had just picked up that song from the airwaves somehow...*

As she heads to the bathroom to brush her teeth and wash her face the music transitions into Barry White's "Can't Get Enough Of Your Love Baby." It takes seconds from the opening beat to the beginning of "I've heard people say..." for her to give in to the song's rhythm and as she brushes away she makes a small wish, that wherever he is, wonder finds him and he knows she is thinking of him.

All in all it takes her roughly 3 and 1/2 hours from that moment which she calls the beginning of her "good morning sunshine routine" to the moment she arrives at her small studio. Three hours are used for getting ready: which roughly means going through teeth brushing, a little bit of stretching, a little bit of dance, a quick breakfast mostly comprised of mango —ataulfo preferred — and a seven minute egg sprinkled with pepper, her daily morning room clean up, the minutes spent packing up the pieces of the project she brought home, and the minutes needed to grab everything she needs before heading out.

The rest of the time is then spent getting to her studio that is technically close by. Technically because while on a map it is just a few blocks away, the concept of close changes depending on traffic. Normally she gives herself more time to try a different route to work and bump into something unexpected, today however, she is trying to keep her focus on the things she wants to accomplish and thus — hopefully— leave little room for daydreams. Her focus is so consumed that she fails to realize today is Saturday and while she does need to be at the studio, traffic is far lighter at this time and it will be at least an hour before D shows up to shoot her audition.

She sighs and unpacks her tablet and the white rose raspberry tea she brought for the pantry. She turns on her speakers and presses play on her latest musical melange. Marvin Gaye's "Ain't No Mountain High Enough" starts playing in the background. The part of her that silently complains at the prospect of days without daydreams she now quenches with music. What started out as a couple of songs that helped her stay focused and awake, has now become a long set of multi-genre melodies that accompany her day to day and keep her grounded through time and space. Little did she know as she was building this playlist that — when you listened to it closely — the pieces on the playlist itself continuously brushed each moment with (that) dreamlike magic. This realization had been a sweet surprise, something she deeply relished every time she pressed play as a signal that everything was going to be alright.

She opens her files and looks at the heavily coordinated "to-do" list otherwise known as the constant lifesaver in her current state of distraction. The morning sun is still coming through with gentle light, its warmth reaches her cheek and she smiles as she remembers the comforting feeling of his grin next to hers. She shakes her head, takes out a small usb, and walks across the room to where her own project is underway letting the beginning of Olivia Newton John's "Magic" dissolve into the background. It is in that manner that her sister finds her an hour later.

"Did you borrow grandpa's playlist or something?" D asks as soon as she walks in.

"Or something," she responds. Pedro Infante's "Deja Que Salga La Luna" is playing its last verse. "Just borrowed a few songs. Give it a moment."

Sure enough as the last beats fade out the beginning drums of "Te Mando Flores" follows.

"Ok, Fonseca is in there too? What gives?"

"I started a new playlist to keep my mind from daydreaming, lo and behold it's all like that."

"Still having trouble with your dreams?" D, who wants to be supportive of her sister's point of view, tries not to frown but her face has always been a ready canvas for *all* her thoughts (emphasis on *all*).

"More like having trouble with my inability to remember them lately. I keep getting sprinkles of moments. It's getting confusing so I'm trying to avoid dreaming and daydreaming. I'm trying to avoid it so much so that I forgot today was Saturday." She sighs, lowers the music with her little remote, and grabs the camera on her desk. "Ready?"

"You good?"

She pauses for a moment before answering, "Yeah, I think I am."

"That doesn't sound too reassuring. You never pause, your answers are always at the tip of your tongue long before I am finished with my questions."

"I am good, I've been keeping myself busy and focused that's all. It's just sometimes I can't help but wonder... sometimes when I wake up I feel like I spent the night talking to a star, and I wonder... Is it the light in the past that is traveling years to find me to tell me something? Is it the present that is breaching through space to give me hope? Or is it the future showing me there is a clear way forward? A road to follow? I don't know. I just know no matter how hard it has gotten to remember clearly — and no matter how fantastical it sounds — these dreams have been a little piece of heaven shining down on me and I can't shake the feeling there is something there I am not supposed to forget. Something I can only believe in and hope it shows itself to me somehow. Anyway, it's no use talking about it. All in all I am good."

"Hmmm. I think talking about it is exactly what you need." D looks around at her sister's project, "What's all this?"

"My latest project."

"I figured as much. What is it called?"

"I am still working out the kinks but Mirror will definitely be in the title."
Her sister walks in front of the projector and sees to her surprise it is an interactive hologram.

"Oh! How did you do this?"

"I've been tinkering with the projector, some filters, and movement recognition software. What do you think?"

"I love it. It's like I am in the painting," says D excited.

"That's the point, you are. I wanted to explore the subject of the muse as more than the passive actor in an artist's portraits, rather as an active ingredient in the making of the piece itself. It's supposed to be an immersive experience in which the person can see how the portrait can change depending on the muse, calling attention to the ingredient that is the muse, and the voice the muse has even in the silence of the painting's surface."

Her sister plays with the features and moves into another painting.

"Would the Mona Lisa smile the same if she were me?" D clicks on the Da Vinci experience, "Ok forest green is definitely not my color, but kudos this is insane."

"Thanks, I'm still finalizing the details but I am very proud of it."

"What are you doing with it?"

"I'm submitting it to a couple of interactive festivals and then showcasing it in a small gallery downtown. I have been thinking about opening my own space."

"Why don't you? You certainly have the content to keep it open. What's this your 5th project this year?"

"7th, but the others are not quite completed yet," she says looking at the cabinet door next to her.

"What's stopping you?"

"I haven't found the right space yet.I want it to have that feeling, you know? Like when you are looking for a house and you find the one that feels like home."

"I know what you mean," D sighs. "Do you have any Magritte in here? That would be a fun one!"

"Not yet!" She laughs as she starts picturing people interacting with a surrealist hologram perhaps with a floating hat and a peering cloud-full eye... *c'est ne pas un mur? ... c'est ne pas un rêve?*

"You are already thinking about it aren't you?" Says D knowingly.

"Yep!" She answers. "It could work, the core of the project is about the relationship between what inspires the artist and what the artist expresses from that inspiration. Even in still life, there is still life."

"Even in still life there is still life," says D still playing with the hologram.

The playlist continues as The Darkness "I Believe In a Thing Called Love," playing it's opening lines. She grabs her phone, and posts the title to her IM-LISTENING stream. It takes all but a few seconds for @willandheart to like her post. She smiles at his response.

"What was that?" Asks D.

"What was what?" Asks G.

"That smile, you are talking to someone aren't you?" Says D

"Oh it is so not what you think. I am just having this musical tête-à-tête with someone on IM-LISTENING," says G laughing.

"Hmmm... ok," says D.

"We just publish songs and sometimes tag songs to each other, and it's become a bit of a conversation."

"You are communicating through songs... I guess it beats dreams, at least this person is flesh and bone," says D shaking her head.

"There is absolutely no point of comparison, it's just fun," She sighs, "Come on let's get you settled. I am hoping we can still use the sun as a kicker. I set up the white and green backgrounds in the Orange room and the Blue Room for you in case you do decide to add a background later."

"Cool. Where do you want me?"

"Is this for the last slides you sent me or the second to last? There was a deadline change on the last one right?"

"The last. That is correct, the last are now priority, but if you have time we may as well do them all today."

"I can do that. Mid-shots or full-body?"

"Mid and flattering please."

"You had to ask?"

"What? Better say than have to re-do them later."

She shakes her head, "Are you using any props for these?"

"No, but I've been thinking about it, they do help sometimes expand the imagination."

"Personally I think not having them can help expand the imagination further, then again it really depends on each actor and what brings out the best in them."

"Well I didn't bring any so I guess I'll have to test out your theory."

"I guess we will," She says smiling, "I'm sure you'll nail it either way. Let's try using the Orange room. We have 2 more hours before we have to head out to brunch. Did you know I almost forgot it was Saturday?" She lowers the volume on her speakers just as Doris Day's "Dream A Little Dream Of Me" starts playing and looks at the flowery coo-coo clock on her wall.

"I can't say I'm surprised. You just told me that."

"Oh. I guess I did. So you are auditioning for a new type of Spaghetti Western?"
D takes the slides out of her bag and gives them to G as they walk over towards the Orange room.

"It's a parody set in the early days of Spaghetti Westerns, just as they start taking shape as alternative content to Italian Art Cinema. I finally watched the movies you recommended by the way."

"And. What did you think?"

"They are stunning. It's like someone placed a roller on — what are you doing?"

"I am making sure you like the first shot. Let me do my thing and you can complain after the shot if you don't like it."

"Fine. Just call action."

She turns off the music. "Action."

Brunch with the girls had become a weekly occurrence. Since spring had come knocking it meant a picnic in the afternoon and a projector with movies in someone's garden. As they walk into A's backyard they realize everyone else has already arrived. There are blankets and pillows on the grass surrounding a circular coffee table covered with aguas frescas, pastries, at least three different salads, and a tiered section of empanadas or as M would call them, pastelitos. A white sheet hangs on the far end of the backyard and an old school projector is ready next to the stack of movies for later.

"There you are!" says N as D and G walk into the backyard.

"We made it!" She says, laughing. She looks at the time on her phone. "Not too bad, I'd say it's a new record."

N laughs and walks over to hug them hello. "You are getting better!"

"Hey!" Says A, coming out of the house with a tray of plates and silverware, "Come get some empanadas before they get cold."

"Or pastelitos," says M.

"Potatoes, Potatoes," says A.

"What's in a name?" replies S.

"Exactly, as long as they are delicious, I am having them," says G.

"Did you get cajeta?" says D.

"You know it!" answers A.

"Come on," says N, "apparently I have missed a whole lot, movies, dreams..."

"Oh you heard?" She sighs.

"You weren't going to tell me? Your oldest and dearest friend?" says N.

"Hey!" says S.

"I've known her since we were thirteen!"

"Fine, I guess I am her younger and dearest friend then," says S enjoying a spinach and feta pie.

"What dreams? What did I miss?" Asks C as they sit down around the table.

"What did we miss? You weren't going to say anything?" Says M.

G proceeds to recount as succinctly as possible what has been going on in her life.

"Wow, I would have trouble waking up," says C.

"Yeah, we've covered that," says D, "Don't encourage her please."

"Where do we sign up for these?" Says N.

"Believe me, if there was a sign up sheet I'd be all over that right now," she sighs, "I haven't had a full dream like that in a while now. Just snippets."

"You know what this reminds me of? Do you remember that movie the 'Lake House' ?" Says C, "Doesn't something like that happen there? Isn't the issue that they are caught in different timelines for a while ?" asks C.

"Yes but one that was a movie, and two they had actual physical proof of the other person's existence," says D.

"You really are not into this are you?" asks N.

"It's a matter of 'how?' Quite simply, 'how?' " says D.

"How? More like why? I'd say," says M.

"Hang on, what if this is exactly like a movie? You know? What if this is all the movies in her subconscious trying to tell her something ?" says S.

"I can get onboard with that. Like 'Contact'," says D, "minus the alien part, just to be clear, let's at least leave the conversation on earth." D turns to G "Wait, weren't you obsessed with that 'Sleeping Beauty' song as a kid?"

"Once Upon A Dream?" She says, "Yeah, I loved that song, still do. It's beautiful."

"Yeah and the lyrics go 'I know you, I walked with you Once Upon A Dream…' isn't it all about them knowing each other in a dream first?" Says D.

"Come on guys, I get the approach but what are we saying here, that my subconscious came up with a collage of my favorite movies to create the perfect scenario for me to fall in love?"

"Maybe? This could be a good thing," says J, "maybe this guy is a total Monet. Dreamy from afar and best appreciated at a distance. If you get too close you'll ruin the illusion."

"I wouldn't care if he looks like a Picasso. With dreams like that I'll have what she is having," says A excitedly.

"I second that!" Says N.

"You say there is music in your dreams? Maybe that means something?" Asks C.

"I am hoping it does," she says.

"If music be the food of love, play on!" Says S.

Play on and on and on... she thinks as she smiles a the thought... "Maybe it is the love of my life," she says, "Maybe it is the beginning of a beautiful friendship? Maybe it's both? Who knows?"

"Isn't that the point?" Says M.

"Alright, if all of you are just going to keep going on with the pop-culture references — yes, I am considering Shakespeare's Twelfth Night a pop-culture reference S— then I think this is a Like vs. Love scenario, you know, you love your sneakers because you don't have a Prada back-pack?" Says D.

"Really?" She says a bit taken aback at the comparison.

"I think it is pretty straight forward, you like your dreams because you don't have the reality. If you had the reality you would love the reality. I think it's the lack of contrast that is making it difficult for you to realize the difference."

She sighs, "It's just not like that. I get it why it would seem so, but it's not. I can't really explain it. It's not out of lack. I wish I had something concrete to help me explain better. Even in the 'Lake House,' when they had the letters and it took a whole universe to bring them together, they connected and it wasn't because they didn't have someone special in their lives it was because they were too special to each other to look or want to look anywhere else. You know?"

"But they didn't have someone special in their lives," says D, "That's the point."

"No, I mean it wasn't about having or not having someone special in their lives, they were just doing their thing when love found them in an unexpected way," says G.

"Yes, but they had letters, you have dreams, they are ephemeral at best," says D trying to put it as gently as possible.

"I know, I know, I know, how it sounds ok? It's just they are too real, and without proof I can't do anything about it but enjoy them and see where they take me," she sighs.

"I still say it reminds me of the 'Lake House,' " says C, "and isn't the whole underlying premise based on 'Persuasion'? "

"I guess it is," she says thinking about the concept of persuasion.

"Look who is to say these dreams you are having aren't trying to tell you something. As long as you are ok, then I say let them tell you what they are trying to tell you," says C.

"What I don't get," says A, "is how, in this day and age, you cannot find a person. I mean do you know his name? His phone number? Email? Socials? It would be so easy to figure this out if you did."

"Exactly," says D, "More to my point that this is a dream."

"I honestly don't know why we haven't talked about that. It's silly I know but it's like we already knew each other so we didn't need to introduce ourselves," she says.

"I mean, I've been there before," says S, "ok not exactly, but it's like when you are at a party and meet someone and immediately hit it off and you don't introduce yourselves until you remember you actually don't know each other's name."

"I don't see the logic there," says D

"Oh come on D, the logic there is that there is something bigger than 'hello my name is' happening, so the 'hello my name is' part goes to the background," says S.

D raises her eyebrows, "I mean once I get, a whole year of conversations is a completely different story..."

"It may not be logical but it beats going to sleep and waking up without a dream in between," says A, "I say enjoy them while they last. Take the endorphins, let them make you happy."

"And we are back to the movie references," says D, "You guys are not helping here."

"If you ask me," says J, "It sounds serendipitous. If it is meant to be then it will be."

"Maybe that's it, maybe it's a matter of serendipity and waiting for everything to align," she says.

"Maybe you met in a past life, and your present life is resolving something unconsciously?

We haven't really explored that possibility," says S smiling at G optimistically.

"Or maybe you just get to meet over the rainbow ?" Says D, "I'm not trying to be the Wicked Witch of the West here, I'm just saying, maybe just maybe this is the place where you get to meet for a specific reason, and it is beautiful but it is only that. You know?"

Maybe, she thinks — *except— except in this scenario that place over the rainbow is the one that feels most like home...*

"We get it," says M turning to D, "You don't think there could be anything real to this."

"It's not that there couldn't be anything real to this, I think it is happening for a reason, but it is her own mind doing it," says D.

"So what do you want to do about it G?" Asks C.

"Something, I am just not sure what there is to do yet," she sighs, "How about we talk about something else? There are a lot exciting things happening in everyone's lives."

"Alright," says A, "how are everyone's New Year's resolutions coming along?"

As everyone gets into the conversation status of the New Year's resolutions they so carefully crafted months earlier, she is left to ponder the heart of the matter, secretly hoping that she could — on demand — go where blue birds fly. As she uncrosses her legs she remembers she is wearing red shoes, *perhaps* she thinks, *perhaps if I tap the heels, perhaps they'll take me to him*... She closes her eyes and discretely gives her heels three taps.

"Are you alright?" Asks D.
She opens her eyes and sighs.

"Yep, yep," she answers as she reaches out for a spinach empanada. *Worth the try...* It's been 10 hours since she woke up, only 6 more to go and maybe, just maybe, she'll see him again and hopefully remember it this time...

The phone in her pocket vibrates and she looks at the screen, she has a new notification, @willandheart tagged her previous post with his own of Journey's "Don't Stop Believing." She smiles thinking *I absolutely will not.*

SUMMER.

Two tiny tears stream down her eyes as she wakes up. It was too early to wake up. Still for some reason she had been pulled from a wonderful dream with him again. *Was she saying goodbye? Why was she crying?* She looks at the window, it's not even dawn yet. She sighs, turns around and goes back to sleep.

Another door. It's has been door after door after door. Where will this one lead? She opens. It leads to a long winding stone hallway, something out of a medieval castle. The heavy stones on the walls carry a cool breeze that adds freshness to an otherwise enclosed space. She looks back. The door is gone, in its stead the hallway continues as if the door only existed to let her pass. She takes a step forward and starts to hear the faint call of music at a distance. She walks towards the music. *This must be a dream,* she thinks to herself. She takes another step and feels the cold stone close to touch. She looks down. She is wearing ballet slippers and the end of a silk pink dress fans at her heals. Gentle streams of sunlight— not unlike the ones that wake her up every morning— catch the bottom of the dress and lead her attention to a window nearby. She walks towards the small simple glass-less opening between the steady stream of stone. The music is loudest here. She looks out the window, all she sees is forest. A light glistens at a distance. A bright color she can't quite make out shines from the forest below, and the music, the music sounds so bright she can almost see the notes forming in the air.

Something covers the window, something pushes her back. Steam follows. She sees a peering eye, she catches her breath. A dragon. The music starts sounding louder and louder. She sees the dragon start to turn its head away from her and towards the music. Without second thought, she whistles loudly to catch the dragon's attention. The dragon's attention returns to her. She knows she has to keep the dragon away from the music. She turns and runs away, whistling as she goes. She can feel the dragon's gaze on her. Somehow, it has found its way inside the corridor. She keeps running, and running, and running, until she sees a corner.

This will buy me some time, she thinks as she turns the corner. She sees another door, she opens it. It is a room with a single bed and a tiny window. She closes the door softly and closes her eyes, hoping for the dragon to simply pass by. She looks out the window, she can still see the forest from there, the notes are still in the air. She hears a loud thump outside the door and opens it to find the dragon's tail covering the entrance. She sighs and closes the door. As she stands behind the door she turns to the window, at least she'll have a bit of music. She slides down the door and onto the floor. She hugs her legs and hides her face between her arms. In doing so she notices her dress has turned blue. She tries to hold back the tears streaming from her eyes but it is no use. They have a mind of their own as if they know a loss she doesn't quite understand. She starts hearing the melody again, *dum da di di, dum da di di*... and just like that she wakes up.

What was that? She thinks. She looks at her alarm, it is time to wake up. She turns up the volume on the song. It had been months now since she began using that song to wake up. She'd heard somewhere that if you have a song stuck in your head the thing to do is listen to it fully and it would help end the loop. That had not been the case. Besides, she had realized at her sigh of relief when it didn't work that she didn't really want to end the loop — she wanted to live in it. She had fallen asleep to the song last night too, *maybe that was what had caused the dream…* she thought. She had looked for the artist a few times and found his art. There were a couple of pictures here and there, she just couldn't be certain it was the same man.

She thought about her hesitation, *was it just doubt at the possibility of it all being real? Was she just filling the blanks with wishful thinking?* She sighed, she just had to wait for her answer. If it was him, he would let her know, she just knew — or maybe hoped — he would let her know.

She shakes her head. At least all the doors made sense. The last few months had been a series of doors. It had been door, after door, after door. Knocking had become a workout at this point. The answers on the other side of the door had simply been a variation on the same theme. They first start with sharp silence — a stark contrast to the emphasis of her knock. After the unequivocal sound of silence came the theme: it is all part of your inner most thoughts, your inner most desires, an explanation from your spirit or subconscious for your conscious self. It didn't matter the title on the door, or the sitting space, the ongoing conclusion was that — yes, it was real — but only for her.

There was the unconventional door here and there that alluded to the possibility of something more. That something more, however, always remained as an allusion — a potential allusion even — be it to protect the utterer in legal matters, be it to easily justify an expertise by not making a mistake, or simply because it was in this open field of alluded possibility that even the improbable had space to exist. If she allowed it any of those explanations could fit in the space the question kept empty. They could fit, they were just not a match. *Everything can have a logic,* she thought, *but not everything can have heart...* and the heart of the matter was what she was looking for.

She looks at her phone, there is a text from N from late last night.

N: "Hike tomorrow? 7am?"

She looks at the time, it is 6:30am.

G: "Usual?" She answers.

N: "Yes! See you in 30?"

G: "Make it 40? (blushing emoji)"

N answers with a thumbs up and a laughing emoji.

A reminder pop-s up on her phone for an Ayahuasca experience tomorrow with her sister. She cringes at the thought. While she wasn't particularly interested in the experience, it wasn't the Ayahuasca or the time with her sister that inspired her reaction, it was the idea of putting herself out there for another answer that left things up in the air. It was becoming a bit too much. She looks at her list. Almost all theories had been crossed out, if they kept going in this direction she would be hiring a ghostbuster and getting an MRI by the end of the month. The whole situation had gotten out of hand. It had become about proving a reality to others instead of just letting it be what it means to her. She knew there was a big difference between what seems and what is and what is always revealed itself, she just had to give it time. This thought seems to settles things for her and so she grabs the phone and texts her sister.

G: "I am throwing away the list! How about a spa day instead?"

D: "YEEESSSS!"

D's level of excitement practically bounced off the text. She hearts D's message, and presses play on her playlist. Harry Style's "Sunflower Vol.6" starts playing in the background. She smiles at the thought of meeting someone after brushing her teeth and posts the song to her IM-LISTENING stream. She notices @willandheart likes the post. The sun is rising, she better start getting ready or she would be more late than usual.

A few hours later N and her are sitting on a big boulder at the top of a luscious mountain. The petunias along the hike trail have started to bloom and soft lilacs and yellows sprout proudly alongside long trails of wispy grass. The air is full and clear — perfect for breathing — and the day is sunny — perfect for feeling. They share a sandwich N pre-packed, along with some apple slices, and their favorite chips. A few packets of Valentina have been opened and the conversation has since dwindled as they looked on at nature in silence.

"You know, ever since I've known you you are always thinking," says N breaking the silence, "You should give that brain of yours a rest."

G laughs, "I know, I can't help it."

N passes her the apple slices, "What's up?"

She sighs, "I was just thinking about the trees."

"They are taking on nicely aren't they?"

"Beautifully."

"It's been nice to work on a project like this, I think I may just start doing this full time."

"It's the best office I've ever seen."

"Right? And you can come visit any time," says N.

"I'll take you up on that. I am glad you are doing what makes you happy," she replies.

"Me too. We are finishing this reforestation project and then heading up to Colorado for the next one. I will be supervising the new trainees. You should come. We can make a week of it and go on an adventure. It's been a while."

"It has, hasn't it? I miss our adventures. When was the last one?"

"When you jumped into the ice pond and thought it was going to be the same temperature throughout," laughs N.

"Hey there were kids swimming there and my feet said it was fine."

"Yes, where there was sunshine! You plunged into the deep end."

"Oh I remember, it took two seconds for my body to yell 'abort, abort' ! "

"I know," N laughs more at the memory, "That was fun."

"I'll just pack a wetsuit next time."

"Seriously?"

"You know I can't pass by a body of water and not want to jump in, that's why I get so frustrated on cruises. Days at sea? More like days observing sea!" She says feeling the frustration.

"So, how's life?" N takes a bite of her sandwich. "I know you weren't only thinking about trees."

She sighs, "Fair. I was thinking about how little we see. I look before me and I see a beautiful forest with lines of trees, yet each of those trees is a home to all kinds of different creatures and they all make a different part of the tree their home. I was thinking that if we could ask, they probably would not describe the tree the same way. If the bird talked about the branches, and the squirrel about the trunk, and the fox about the base of the tree, or the butterflies about anywhere else on the tree — granted I know nothing of bugs — , I am sure they would all express a different home yet they would all be right in their description of the tree. Maybe the bird would not understand the fox, or the squirrel, or vice-versa, but it wouldn't make their experience living in the tree any less real. It wouldn't make their home less real. It is the same tree and they can all call it home without having to change it into what the other animal has in order to prove it is their home too. My point is sometimes you don't need things to be understood by others to mean something to you, and also you don't need things to be the same for everyone to make one thing real or not."

"Ok…" says N, "are you ok?"

"I was thinking about home because I am in love, I am *in* love and I want to live in the space where this love exists. It is not a space I know, or a space I can show, and I don't know what to do about it." She sighs, relieved at finally being able to express out loud what she had wanted to for the last few months.

N thinks for a second, "Well…I think being in love is already doing something."

"True," she drinks from her water. "I may just have to remember that. "

"I am looking forward to being in love again. It's been a while."

"Yes, it has. You are not scared?" she asks remembering her initial reaction.

"What's the point? If I'm in love I'm in love, it's not going to go away because I'm scared, might as well embrace it."

"True. I just have to remember that when we love we heal and sometimes little bruises pop-up here and there as the healing is happening. I don't want to let them define what my heart can feel. You know?"

"Oh yeah, exactly as I would say it," says N smiling, "Only you G, only you. So, when are we doing a double date?"

She laughs, "That I couldn't tell you."

"Aha. It is the dream guy again isn't it?" She nods in silence and turns her head away so her friend doesn't see the little tear that is currently escaping her eye.

She sighs, "I see him everywhere, yet I can't find him anywhere. What am I supposed to do with that? I don't want to let go, I don't think I actually can, yet I also know it would not be wise to hold on to an endless dream I cannot reach. Then I remember the best part of the dream is to believe and do what you can and let the rest follow... and I am back at square one. If there were a thousand ways to love him I'd know them all by heart and I'd still come up with new ones for the times we are apart."

"Look I honestly don't know what to tell you. I can see how difficult this must be for you, to feel something so real for something you are not sure is. All I can say is I know you, and you have a sense of the world that is entirely your own, if there is something there then I say follow your heart and let it take you where you need to go. If there is something you can do just do it and see what happens. I promise if I see you tripping over your own two feet I will say something."

"I promise if you say something I won't disregard it."

N laughs, "That's all I ask. Look whatever this is, it seems to be good for you, you are more … you! If it wasn't the case we would be having a very different conversation." N places her arm around her friend's shoulder reassuringly. "You never know, love has a funny way of making everything better, even if it is hard to see what it is doing. You'll figure out what you can do about it. That creative brain of yours is sure to come up with something to figure this out and I'll be right here. You know we all will."

"You know, there is something I've been going back and forth about. I think I am just going to go for it and give it a try."

"See, figuring it out already!" Says N raising her water bottle in a toasting motion. As they cling their water bottles a hummingbird flies by and stops on the flowers next to her. She can't help but notice its wings. Its wings beat so fast only a streak of transitioning colors can be seen around it, yet they are there in speedy movement while the little bird's body remains absolutely calm taking all the time in the world to enjoy the nectar from the flower. *Time, it is a funny thing...*

FALL

This is home, she thinks as she dances in his arms. What a wonderful feeling that, knowing that there is a space that requires no roof, no walls, no doors, and yet it is home. As she pulls her head from his shoulder to look up at his face, she wakes up. She is in the castle room again, on the bed she has carefully avoided time and time again. She looks around. This time the room has many doors. She opens the first, the dragon's tail is blocking the way. She closes it and opens the next door, the dragon's leg is there. She closes it and opens the next door, part one of the dragon's torso is visibly there, she opens the next door — lo and behold — there is part two, and the next door and part three... *this is one big dragon...*she thinks.

The door after that is blocked by another leg, a front leg she assumes. She stops opening doors when she realizes she is getting dangerously close to the dragon's face. She sighs and goes to the bed. *Could she wake herself up from this?* She hears the music playing at a distance, the sound is getting louder and louder, she closes her eyes and wishes to wake up. *Just wake up,* she thinks, and just like that she wakes up.

At least this time the dress didn't stay blue, she noticed. This time the dress kept going from blue to pink, that must mean something other than an allusion to a "Sleeping Beauty" fantasy. She looks at her alarm clock, it's almost 4pm. She must have dozed off while she worked. Her exhibit is almost done, she just had to finish adding a few details to the road.

"Hello?"

She hears someone call out by the door. *Did I have an appointment?* She can't quite remember. It has been a blur of a week. She stands up from her work station and walks towards the main room hosting the exhibit. The frame to a house stands tall in the center, a thin organza fabric covers the top of the room dipping slightly in the middle and extending to the corners of the frame with streaks of yellow and gold cascading down as sun-rays. A tree made up of paper holds one of the house's beams. It branches out towards the side and front, shading the entire right side of the house with jacaranda blooms that snow down sporadically sprinkling the floor with gentle blue hues. Small round fluffy clouds made of foam are stationed throughout the room connecting to the walls and floor. They allow visitors a comforting and bouncy sitting space. The walls are painted with gentle white and blue shades, the brushstrokes purposefully visible and the evolving colors in them still unblended.

A blue bird hologram seemingly lands on one of the back tree branches, a second blue bird appears next to it as the light on the wall indicates the sun is rising. A soft instrumental melody plays in the background filling the space in between with hope and magic. *Almost there*, she thinks. She walks towards the entrance where giant papier-mâché sunflowers stand tall and bright, facing one direction as a friendly welcome committee.

"Hello," she says as she opens the door. She freezes on the spot. A man is standing there, his back to her. He is wearing a long coat, his hair is disheveled — *just like his,* she thinks— her heart skips a beat. Without realizing it she takes a step towards him, her hand reaches out to touch his back. She catches herself in time, shakes her head, takes a deep breath, and repeats, "Hello?"

He turns around. *It's not him*, she thinks. *Of course it's not him*, she repeats to herself.

"Hi, I am here for the review." Says the man.

"Oh, that's right. I wasn't expecting you until tomorrow morning," she says.

"Yes, my colleague was supposed to come by tomorrow but there was a last minute change. They asked me if I could cover it and I could only do it tonight. I am sorry I thought they called you."

"They might have, I have terrible reception here," she smiles, "It's alright, I am glad I was here. I can show you around. If you can stay the hour you will see the space transition from day to night. It cycles by the hour," she says as she motions for the man to follow her, "Everything is pretty much done, I am just finishing the road you see here." She points to an acrylic stream-like road that leads to the house. The edges have been filled in with yellow quilling in the shape of breadcrumbs.

"The installation itself is meant to be a space for dreamers," she continues, "It is about believing in the impossible, about loving with all your heart, and remembering what makes you live fully."

"Interesting, what made you think of that?" He points towards the cloud-like sitting areas in the corners.

"Oh," she smiles, "sometimes it is only in dreams where we believe in the impossible, but in reality the difference between the impossible and the improbable is only a matter of creativity and will. Take these chairs for example, you and I can look at the sky and wish to touch the clouds, and maybe we cannot do it as birds do, however, we can find our own unique way to touch them. The important thing is to allow the dream to inspire the journey. The chairs are clouds you can sit on, because dreams are something you can build on."

"Is there something written in these clouds?" The man points at the clouds on the wall, "There seems to be a movement to them. Was that on purpose or a stream-of-consciousness piece of artistry?"

She smiles "Good eye! Yes, if you stand over here and turn very slowly clockwise, you will see." She leads him away from the main wall and points towards the area where the ceiling and the walls meet. From the corner of the room the beginning of the sentence forms, and if you turn around slowly you can distinguish the letters that make a short love note in the clouds. They read:

"Where there is a will there is a way, and where there is love there is always a will."

"I can see it!"

"I wanted to create a space that could cross the line between the quotidian and the magical. Something that would bring alive — if only for a moment — the wonders people feel when they are watching a fantastical space like Oz, Wonderland, Narnia, or even the Wonka Factory. Please," she points towards the far left corner of the room where the space gently morphs into a small hilltop with flowers blooming at the sides. As they reach the tromp d'oeil space, the idyllic hilltop picnic area reveals itself to be a table.

"You see, to me, the sweetness of the dream is very much like the sweetness of a loving kiss. It is filled with promise that only needs to be cherished and nurtured to bloom," she touches a flower and the flower opens up gently to reveal a candy inside, "Would you like some?"

"Very, very, Wonka of you. How did you manage that?"

"It's a secret, but I will share this, the basis is origami and all of the treats are from third party suppliers — local manufacturers, personal favorites — you can find the information for their business if you visit the QR code on the wrapper. "

"Fascinating. May I?" The man says reaching out to grab a star shaped gummy.

"Please. May I offer you something to drink as well?" She asks. "I am afraid I can only offer you water right now, but tomorrow we will have orange Jarritos and green tea as well."

On either side of the hilltop, just where it meets the wall, are three painted trees with poking burls. She grabs a small cup from a stack that until now had been completely dissimulated as part of the trunks. She places the cup at the left edge of the creek and presses on one of the burls on the left-sided tree. A steady rivulet of water comes down the left side of the creek and onto the cup. A little closer look reveals the creek is divided down the middle, effectively leading each side of liquid to its intended destination upon request.

"Each line of liquid connects to its own cooler at the back, rest assured I have undergone the proper inspection and can show you all the paperwork if needed." She says as she gives him the cup with water.

"I appreciate that." He says inspecting the cup and placing it in front of it's place of origin to explore the connection. The liquid has changed the color pattern slightly so to make it distinguishable from the other empty cups.

"It's on purpose." She offers the explanation, "Contrast is important. This cup is filled, those are empty," she says pointing at the stacked cups. "The paper on the cup changes hue slightly with temperature to make it easy to distinguish one from the other."

"Fantastique! Ok, I do not wish to ruin the experience for visitors. Do you mind if I keep the pictures only to the sunflowers at the entrance? I feel like this space needs to be experienced."

"I would appreciate that actually. Thank you."

In what to her seemed like a matter of minutes the space was suddenly filled with enthusiastic onlookers. As the clock marks 8pm she turns her eyes towards the ceiling. A shooting star was set to cross the night sky on the hour. *Do you know what that point is on the horizon?* His words echo in her heart … She was savoring the memory, thinking… *perhaps I could have added a plane on rotation…* when she heard someone explaining the exhibit to another.

"It's like that too, you know?" said the one to the other, "It's like this space, it's alive, because you can't plan the perfect moment, but you can let the perfect moment happen if you are open to it." *They are right,* she thought to herself, she just needed to let the moment happen.

"Let me guess, inspired by a dream or two?" Says D

"Maybe…" she turns to welcome D and J.

The space has been open for an hour now and it has been packed with visitors. The opening night was proving a success.

Her sister sighs and shakes her head, "Well now I see why you didn't want to leave your dream-space."

"Go check out the snack table. You will love it!" She says pointing towards the hilltop.

"It's good!" Says N walking towards them and unwrapping a blueberry Bubbaloo, "I like what you did with this space G." N nods towards the message in the night sky.

Following the shooting star's trail, words subtly appear written in the stars beyond forming that which resembles a wave-like constellation. They flash gently on for 14 minutes to give the onlookers enough time to make them out, and reappear after the next shooting star cycle. The words read: *"If there were a thousand ways to love you I would know them all by heart, and I'd still come up with new ones for the times we are apart..."*

"You came up with new ones alright!" Says N, "I have to say this is not what I expected when you said you had an idea you wanted to try."

"What can I say, even in dreams love inspires," she says, "whatever this has been, whatever he has been — is — this, all this, will always be a beautiful inspiration to live and love."

"Now, that was inspired," a new voice shared.
N and G turn around to see a young woman with thick red framed glasses smiling at them.

"There is a story here isn't there?" the lady says, "It feels like a story that needs to be told. Have you considered writing it?" The lady's phone starts to ring. N and G look at each other. "I have to leave, but if you ever decide to write this give me a call." The lady hands her a card and with a heartfelt "congratulations," leaves.

"That is not a bad idea" says S who arrived just at the end of the exchange.

"I'd want to read it too," says C arriving next, "This is wonderful."
G looks at the card. She hasn't written in a while... maybe if she did, maybe it would reach him and let

him know where she was… *Dum da di di di, dum da di di di…* Her heart hiccups at the sound. She looks at her phone, it is not her. She looks around. It was someone's ringtone.

"Hey, have you seen this?" says A handing G her phone. "What are the odds? The song you like and the bluebirds flying into the sunrise."

G looks down to find it is the music video to the song — the song — there is a blue bird flying into a sunrise and *him,* he is running towards the camera! Her heart starts pounding so loud she is sure everyone can hear it blooping. She remembers her words: *If you send this signal I will find a way to answer. I'll know this is real and I will find a way to meet you half way. I promise…*

G looks down at the card in her hand. *She could write to him…*even as she thinks it she knows it is not a question, she will write to him and hope this will be the only door left to open.

A soft instrumental arrangement to *Once Upon A Dream* starts playing in the background. As she thinks about the story she will write, she can faintly overhear S and M talking about a recent movie they watched where the main character is convinced a book written is about her and she goes to find the author only to discover that while the book was not about her, the author turns out to be her perfect match. *That's not it...* she thinks, *I am sure that is not this... Why can't I just find a way to contact him directly? ... surely there must be a way... and then what?... 'Hi, I've been dreaming about you for quite some time now...' I mean things indicated he had been dreaming about her too right? ... right? ...* No, she had to answer with a breadcrumb, if it was real then he would know what it was... he could hear her, surely he would know what it was... it would be discrete and it would be easier for him to reach her now... he would answer... she hoped... she looks down at the card in her hand, she would write to him... *that I can do ...*

As soon as she gets home, the anticipation of the decision made earlier tries to escape her body in bounds of giddiness. She grabs her phone and presses play on her playlist. Abba's "SOS" starts playing and with a laugh at the synchronicity of the moment she posts it to her IM-LISTENING stream in an attempt to get some help from the universe. She still needs to figure out the "how" to do it. She knows that a clear mind is always helpful to find the best way forward so she starts taking care of the small tasks that could distract her with their pending status. Her phone vibrates, @willandheart answered her post tagging her with Rhianna's "Umbrella." She smiles, finds Tina Turner's "Simply The Best" and tags right back.

She then proceeds to get ready for bed. *What am I doing?* She thinks as she brushes her teeth, *there is no reason to postpone this*. Excitement fills her. For a moment she tries to mistake it for dread, but the steadfast beating of her heart soon gives way to an unmistakeable smile that spreads on her face and refuses to leave. Clarity befalling her, she walks up to the desk. Once there she opts for grabbing a pen and notebook instead. Perhaps the gentle movements of the ink on the page will ease the sparks that surround her. With a deep breath she sits down and beings:

"The place is deserted. Long spaces of green gently blown by a cool breeze set the stage..."

1...2...3...

WINTER

She wakes up in the castle room, the song

is louder this time, a small bluebird appears on her

window and looks straight at her for a moment

before flying away. She sits up excited. *This is new*,

she thinks. This time she remembers she has a

choice in these dreams too. She closes her eyes

and asks *I need to find a way through*. The sound of

stones moving catches her attention and she opens

her eyes. An open doorway has appeared on what

moments ago was the far right wall of the room.

She goes to it. A winding staircase leads up. She

follows. She realizes she has reached the top of the

tower when a gust of wind makes its appearance.

Just a few more steps and she will be immersed in

sunlight.

The small circular opening that is the

tower top allows her to see far into the forest. She

can see the clearing of her dreams. There, in the

middle of the clearing, stands a house. Music notes

come up from its chimney. She smiles, it's him. As

the music grows louder she worries the dragon

may awaken from its sleep. She looks down, she

can see the castle clearly now. It is not a castle but

a maze — a labyrinth — and the dragon covers all the entrance points. *There is a way*, she thinks, *labyrinths are never what they seem*. Her heart starts pounding with excitement, he is there, in the house. Her head starts thumping with all the reasons she should be afraid. The music comes back, it's their song. All the reasons on why she should be afraid spiral around in thought, yet in that instant none of them matter anymore, none of them were as real as him — none of them are as real as him. She knew no matter how many reasons scared her she only needed one to keep going, and she knew she loved him more than she could ever be afraid of anything. She just had to make sure the dragon didn't follow her.

  She rushes down the stairs and back into the room. Her dress transitions from pink to blue so fast it seems as if it has forgotten how to be a single color. She reaches the bedroom door and takes a deep breath. *Just because things are scary, doesn't mean you have to be afraid*, she tells herself. She opens the door again, the dragon's tail is still there, but when she looks closely there is an opening to the side with enough room for her to pass through. She does. Making a silent mental note to thank her subconscious for the ballet slippers, she quietly moves past the dragon's tail and onto the hallway without arousing the dragon's suspicion. She keeps walking, keeping her steps light, her feet steady, and trying as hard as she can to keep her breathing gentle. As she turns around the corner she sees the torso (part one) and the door she could not get out from before. Again, there was room for her to pass. She holds back a giggle. She keeps going, grateful that the dragon remains asleep.

She continues until she sees the edge of the dragon's head and pauses for a moment to take a deep breath. She hadn't taken notice of the dragon at all, the thick translucent scales that cover its body seemed particularly sharp around the neck. She braces herself for heat. As she walks towards the face she accidentally slips and falls on the dragon's ear. She covers herself expecting an attack. Nothing happens. She opens her eyes, the dragon's eye looks at her and she realizes it is the only part of the dragon she has seen move. She takes a closer look and sees that the rest of the dragon is covered in a thick stone-like glaze. Frozen in time. She looks forward. There is a clear opening between the dragon's face and the door. She reaches for the door. It is a heavy door. She pushes the door open, it creaks a little, a ray of sunshine comes through and quickly disappears. She looks up. She is staring straight into the dragon's eyes. It seems as surprised as her. She pushes the door a little more and then a little more, slowly letting more light in.

As she leans in with her whole body to open the door fully she feels a strong force pushing the door away from her hands and opening it completely. It is the dragon. It pushed the remaining part of the door open. She looks at the dragon, its scales are now glasslike, glistening lavender and lilac in the sunlight. The dragon passes past her and lays its head at her feet in a silent invitation to ride it. She gets on and without saying anything, the dragon lifts her up and flies her towards the forest. As soon as they land she knows where the dragon has taken her. As she descends from the dragon's back she notices the music has gotten louder. She looks down at her feet, a trail of breadcrumbs ends where she stands. She looks up to see how far it goes. The line continues towards a corner. *Does it end?*

She looks back to thank the dragon but it is gone. She returns her attention towards the breadcrumb trail and follows it. The trail continues until it reaches the clearing, wild pink roses and daisies grow all around. In the center stands the house. A lovely melody comes from it. The breadcrumbs lead all the way to the front door. She smiles. Her heart starts to beat to the music's rhythm. As she walks towards the house she can see him on his guitar playing the melody she knows by heart. She reaches the door. She is about to knock when she notices her sleeve and realizes her dress has turned a steady stream of lavender. He opens the door.

"Welcome home darling!"
A million smiles gather in the corner of his lips just waiting for some subtle mischief or a tender kiss to be let out. She laughs in relief, and as she reaches out to kiss that corner she wakes up.

Yey! she thinks, *should she read into this?*
She looks around at her desk. Notes and notes
from the last year cover her writing wall. Research,
experiences, dreams, studies, anything that had to
do with the exhibit. It must be because the novel
was finished, *yes*, she tells herself, *that's it.* She
looks at the cursor on her screen, it's beating right
where she left it between "love" and "you." She
must have read the story ten times already and
adding the end period had been the only thing
alluding her. How do you end a story that is just
beginning? She sighs and finishes the story the only
way she knows how, with three dots...

She hits command-s for a quick save,
attaches it to the email she left ready, and presses
send. She had gone back and forth changing dots
and words so many times she had to come up with
a way to just follow through when she was finished
and send the piece before she started re-evaluating
minuscule details. Having ensured no dillydallying,
she then quickly turns to the copyright page she
left open, uploads and submits the latest draft, and
checks both items of her to do list. Then, with a
good little stretch she grabs her phone to catch-up

on what the rest of the world has been up to. She undoes the "do not disturb" on her phone, and sees she has a missed phone call from her sister, a reply to her contract from L (she had decided to buy the exhibit space, it felt like home… or rather it had become the space closest to feeling like home), and a notification for a post from @willandheart for Bob Marley's "Don't Worry About A Thing." She smiles as she likes the post and answers the tag with The Monkey's "I'm A Believer." She then calls her sister back.

  As she waits for her sister to answer she looks at the Mafalda poster on her wall. It was a once a neatly folded poster size cartoon that came with the latest Mafalda book her mom gave her. It has since been colored with neon hues and framed in more color. The image has Mafalda looking up at the sun and thinking *"To think that this sun is the same sun that illuminated Shakespeare … and Pasteur!"* . Her sister sends her to voicemail, she must be at another audition. She hangs up and makes a mental note to try again later. She walks over to the poster and turns to look out the window towards the sun. *Mafalda is right, it is the same sun that in its singularity manages to always bring to every individual exactly what they need... it is the same one sun... and yet somehow, when he shows up, the it is always brighter...*

To think it had been months now since she started writing. The beginning was the easy part, figuring out the details, that was challenging. *What to keep in? What to keep out? What to say?* She remembered a college teacher's advice, "write what you know." That proved interesting. To anybody but her — *and him* she thinks— this would be a work of fiction, nevertheless, writing what she knew was a good way to start. Once she decided that, she came to find that it was naming her characters that bemused her. She settled for single letters that could hold a reference point for readers and yet hold her secret in truth.

She reaches for her almond matcha latte, it's colder than she expected. She hadn't noticed the air had gotten a little chilly. She grabs the sweater from behind her chair and as she puts it on she remembers a faint dream conversation about how wearing soft sweaters is like having a warm hug around you... that had been happening a lot lately. Little moments with snippets of conversations that must have happened all those nights she couldn't remember have started to surface. She laughs. To think all she had to do was write their story. Had she known, she would have done it sooner. Then again, she could only say it was their story now, because now she knew it was real. She only hoped he still felt the same way. The answer was on its way. She closes her eyes, hoping he will hear her and sends him a message: *"My answer is on its way, I am coming home."*

She smiles and opens her eyes to see a red heart shaped balloon floating away into the sunset... *huh*... she thinks... Gloria Gaynor's version of "You're Just Too Good To Be True," starts trumpeting in the background, she grabs her phone and posts it to her IM-LISTENING stream. She looks at the time, the little French cafe at the Grove will be filling up soon.

She texts her sister,

G: "Hey, would you like to go for some fondue? Our usual? I'm heading out for a walk. Text me and I'll meet you there."

She grabs a pen and one of the small notecards with orange tulip decals she got last week. She writes something quickly, folds the note gently and puts it in her back jean pocket as she grabs her bag from behind her chair and heads for the door. As soon as she is out of her building her sister texts her.

D: "Hey! Love Fondue! Are you close by?"

G: "I'm walking over. You?"

D: "I'm around the corner from you, want me to pick you up?"

G: "I just want to do something first, want to come with?"

D: "What is it? I hunger. Just finished a dance class."

G: "It's quick, I just need to find a balloon."

Just as she says that her sister sees a store with a big opening celebration banner and balloons on the doors. The lady working there is putting away the colorful chalkboard stand that holds a "Welcome" greeting. D quickly rolls down the window.

"Hey!" D waves at the lady clearing up.

The lady comes over, "Can I help you?"

"Hi! This may be an odd question but what are you doing with those balloons? I see you are about to close. Any chance I could buy one from you?"

"We are. I'll give them to you. We were going to trash them."

"Perfect! Thank you so much!"
The lady goes over to the door to unfasten the balloons as D texts her sister.

D: "I've got your balloons babe! Pick you up in 10 do not move. Just tell me where you are at."

G: "I love you, I love you, I love you. I'm right by the ice cream place we like, the one with the custom made waffle cones."

D: "Done, see you in five."

Five minutes later her sister picks her up on the side of the street, 4 big pink heart-shaped balloons float happily outside the back windows. She smiles and shakes her head, *maybe this will work after all...*

"Thank you, thank you, thank you."

"Ok, so the stars are aligned for you or something. I literally saw them the second you said you needed a balloon and they were free!"

"Lucky me!"

"Now spill." Says D with a smile on her face.

"Remember how when we were little we used to send our letters via balloon to Santa Clause?"

"Yes... wait, is this like a message in a bottle?"

She sighs, it is so much easier when she doesn't have to explain herself, she already knows how it sounds out loud. "Yes. I just finished the novel ——."

"You finished! This is huge, why didn't you say so?"

"I just did!"

"Right, continue."

"I just finished and there's one last thing I'd like to do before releasing the story to the world."

"What are you talking about? Have you seen how happy you've been since you started writing again?"

How do I tell her that the happiness she saw had as much to do with the content as it had to do with the writing? "I want to put something out there into the universe and let it find whomever it needs to find. That's what the balloons are for, or well balloon, the others are just a happy coincidence."

"Alright! Let's make it rain pink—You know what I mean..."

D turns the corner into the parking lot right by the French place they love. As luck would have it, and they happily noticed, a spot opened for them right across the French place. As they get the balloons out of the car, they decide to walk over towards the little grass on the extended sidewalk to release them, just to avoid ongoing traffic and, well, questions. Her sister grabs the balloons. Her fingers touch the note on her pocket and she makes a little silent wish — that the note finds its intended destination. As she takes the note out, a winter gale blows the letter out of her hand and before she can grab it again it swirls it away.

"Oh no!"

"I have pen and paper in the car," says D. She looks around. The note is completely out of sight and she cannot help but smile.

"I wanted to send something where it needed to go, maybe things didn't go as planned but perhaps the note found the wind it needed anyway," she says.

Her sister hands her a balloon. "Here, there is an odd comfort that comes from having one of these in hand."

"Thanks," she takes the balloon, "These are nice to hold. You are right."

"I keep telling everybody. Glad you've caught on."

She laughs, "Come on, let's fondue!"

"We are bringing the balloons?"

"Good point, on the count of three we set them free: una, dos, tres!"

They let go of the balloons.

"Did you make a wish?" Asks D.

"We are sprinkling the sky with extra love, anyone that sees these can make a wish."

"Ok, for that level of cheese I need fondue. Come on," says D, "Oh by the way, I go you something." D takes out a couple of tickets from her jacket pocket.

Her heart starts beating fast. She turns the tickets around.

"I couldn't find any concert tickets for his show yet, but I thought this could be the next best alternative?" Says D.

She looks down at her hand and her smile widens, her sister had gotten her two tickets to the "Sleeping Beauty" ballet.

"This is perfect," she says reaching out for a hug. "Thank you!"

"You are welcome!" D tries to wiggle out from under the hug while G keeps hugging her.

"You are coming with me right?"

"Obvi!" Says D "Now come on, I'm starving!" G let's go of the hug and gives her sister a kiss on the cheek.

As they walk towards the French cafe in conversation four pink heart-shaped balloons reach for the skies, and the note keeps on flying until it reaches someone's face.

He turns it over:

"To You – the man in my dreams – I was scared of the view that comes with a hurting heart, so I forgot of the wonders life brings with a brand new start. Thank you for being the angel of my dreams and reminding me of all the beauty left to touch in reality. Wherever this finds you and I hope it does, may it find you happy, blessed, and home. I love you always…"

He looks around trying to find the owner. He is alone on the street. It was an oddly quiet walk, exactly what he needed. Perhaps this note belonged to one of the drivers passing by… everyone seemed to be too busy heading somewhere to notice a flying piece of paper… He takes the note, reads it again, and smiles as he carefully puts it in his coat pocket. *The universe may be smiling at him after all,* he thinks…

SPRING

"What do you think?" He asks as he turns around to face her. They were sitting at the piano, her head had been resting softly on his shoulder as he finished playing her a new song.

"I love it," she says. She can feel his fingers gently placing a loose strand of hair behind her ear. The tender caress meant to catch her attention transfixed them both. They stare into each other's eyes for a moment. She can see he is tired.

"I've been looking for you," he says.

"I know, I know that now," she answers. She holds his hand to hers, "I am on my way to you, I promise."

Dum da di di di... She doesn't want to wake up but she knows she has to. He is back in her life. She can feel it. The same wonder that used to sprinkle her nights and days had now expanded into an all day universe of loving warmth. This time she will keep it to herself. Whatever happens, she will let it happen on its own and just enjoy the little moments they have together. He was starting to come into focus again. She could hear the sound of his voice so clearly, she could feel his touch, she could remember again. It was real. It had to be.

There were things in life that weren't half as real as these memories. She would know soon enough. She'd done what she could think to do, all she had to do now was hope.

P's little paw finds her face letting her know it's too early to wake up. She was dog-sitting for her sister, although taking care of P was something she readily volunteered for. P had the cheeriest and loveliest disposition all expressed in a little bundle of joy and big warm soulful almond shaped eyes. The song continues to ring. P looks up at her, her big eyes asking in silence for the sound to be turned off so she can continue sleeping. She turns off her alarm. P turns her head back to the pillow and continues to sleep. She gives P a little kiss and gently rolls off the bed, careful not to make a dent — or P will slide into the slot.

She had arrived home last night to a very happy puppy waiting for her. With her tail wagging and a pink sprinkles donut toy in her mouth, P knew that whenever she stayed with G, play time was a guarantee, and it was an absolute joy to see her bouncing up and down on all fours as she dashed from one side of the bed to the other,

moving all the cushions and pillows out of the way
to wiggle her way through into a little fortress. You
had to give her a minute before she stuck her head
out of the pillow combo and pop-ed up in a 'hi-
hello!' ... and then playtime would resume.

Her phone falls to the floor. She looks
down at it, there are new texts in the group chat
and a new post from @willandheart of Whitney
Houston's "I Want To Dance With Somebody" she
likes the post, presses play and answers the post
with Fred Astaire's "Dancing Cheek 2 Cheek." She
then opens the group chat to messages from her
sister and S that say exactly the same thing: "How
did it go?!"

Good question... She thinks back on the last
24 hours. The story had been a success and her
now agent had introduced her to a couple of
people who wanted to turn it into a movie. She was
just pitched a movie version. The elements were in
the pitch but the premise was completely
transformed to make it about virtual reality. It was
an interesting concept to be sure — set in outer
space — but she still could not understand why it
had been so important to make it about anything

other than dreams. *Is dreaming outdated? Perhaps it is easier to believe in what can be quantifiable and controlled,* she thinks, *it doesn't make it any more real, it just makes it controlled and I guess repetitive?* She ponders... *food for thought to continue with later...*

She runs the pitch through her mind one more time. A very eager screenwriter is describing the story:

"Just picture it with me — allow me to walk you through this story — and if you don't like it we will scrape it and explore something else."

"Ok," she'd said open minded.

"Two astronauts in outer space. One makes a call on the radio, 'Houston do you copy? Houston, we have a problem. Houston. do you copy?' No answer. Suddenly the radio picks up another signal from another radio nearby. The person on the other end says 'Hello? Are you there?' , 'Hello? Houston? ' asks the first astronaut. 'No, I thought you were,' the second astronaut answers. 'No. Where are you?' says the first astronaut. 'I am on the planet E, I was finishing a mission with my rover when we had a malfunction... where are you?' asks the second astronaut. 'I am not sure, I lost access to my coordinates,' says the first astronaut to which the second astronaut replies 'I can help, I can send you mine and you can come to me. We can figure this out together.' They talk each other through it and finally when they are about to meet they get radio signal to stay put, Houston is sending help. Just as they are about to be picked up, he asks her out, 'Hey maybe when we are back on earth we can grab a cup of coffee or tea or something?' he says. 'Yes, that sounds nice' she answers. Just then they get beamed up to their spaceships.

The screen stays on outer-space for a moment and then a big banner in neon green letters flashes the words MISSION ACCOMPLISHED. That's when the camera zooms out and we see astronaut one — or two — whichever, taking off their VR equipment and as they do they bump into someone. 'Sorry,' he says. 'No problem,' she answers. They recognize each other's voice and turn around in an instant! They look at each other in surprise and say 'It's you' in unison... And we leave it there for the audience to put together after. Of course, we can intertwine the rest of the story with the mission and VR games... it's just an idea, what do you think?"

I am still thinking about it... she thinks, as she grabs the phone to answer her sister.

G: "I am still thinking about it. Going for a quick run before the dress fitting, have you put in your miles today? "

D: "Not yet. I was just heading out with A. Want to join?"

G: "Should I bring P? By the way, how was your night?"

D: "I'll tell you all about it! May I go get P after? I'm at a 15 minute mile range now, I think it may be too much for her. Where are you at?"

G: "Good point. I am almost at the 16 minute mile mark. FYI I am not sure I will run the entire marathon, I found a system where you sprint 1 minute and walk 3 and I am really liking it. I may also get a t-shirt that says Runner In Training... "

Her sister sends her 3 laughing emojis.

She looks up at P completely asleep and snaps a picture of her for her sister.

G: "I think she would prefer it that way anyway. See you at the park in 15."

She hears her sister heart the last message as she fills P's bowls with breakfast and water.

"I'm here," she says 5 hours later as she enters A's "Petite Atelier"— a small couture made-to-order boutique she opened a few months ago. The sign on the entrance says "Private Event," as the girls get their bridesmaid dresses fitted for J's wedding.

"You're late!" Says A through a mouthful of pins.

"I'd wait to criticize until the pins are out of my mouth," she says smiling as S hands her a champagne glass, "Thanks!"

A puts the last pin in on N's dress, "Ok, now I can say it. You are late!"

"I know. I had a call from my agent about the pitch and lost track of time. Then I bumped into M on the way out and we had a little overdue catch up. I'm sorry. Where's C ?" she asks.

"Just left," says S.

"Phoey, I have her book. Oh, well," she says as she looks for a place to sit.

"Did you just say 'phoey' ?" Asks A.

"I was just about to ask that!" Says N.

"Yeah, it was an 'a phoey' moment for me, I considered 'rats' for a moment but 'phoey' felt more appropriate," she answers as she looks at the open fabric catalogue on the coffee table in front of her. "What's this A?"

"The decorator sent me that catalogue. I am unhappy with the way the wallpaper looks, we need something cleaner so the collections stand out more," says A without looking away from marking N's dress.

"May I?" She asks before turning the page.

"Sure, just put a post-it on that page."

"These are super cute!" Says G.

"And they are made from regenerated yarn!"

"And I love it!" She says as she puts a neon green post-it on the current page and turns the pages. A cream colored fabric with a pink pineapple-outline print catches her attention.

"Ok, I am loving this!" She says excited.

S comes closer, "That looks fun. What for?"

"I would add it to my room. There is something about it, it says to me 'I'm cozy and bright' and probably delicious if I were able to cut it," she says.

"Hungry?" Laughs N.

"Little bit," she says as she takes a picture of the wallpaper information and returns the book to the page A had it at. "Hey, did you know pineapples are considered a type of berry?"

"I did not know that," says S "You learn something knew every day."

"I know!"

"Hey, what did you decide to do about the movie?" Says D changing the conversation.

G takes a seat in a seemingly uncomfortable couch behind her that to her delight turns out to be quite comfy. After taking a pisco-moment to enjoy her realization she continues the re-telling of her conclusion regarding the film matter... "I've had enough time to think about it and I think it changes the story completely, but I did think of a way to incorporate it into the story itself. You know how I talk about the stars and dreams? I added a little something to make room for the astronauts. Anyway I hope that they are interested in my edit, if not I'll just wait for the right person to work with on this. Did you know astronaut means 'star sailor' in greek?"

"Oh no, don't you start!" Says D.

"Well that fits then!" Says S laughing.

"Don't get too comfortable G! You are next," says A without turning away from the dress in her hands, "Your dress is in dressing room 3."

"Alright, I'm on it," she says as she stands up and heads towards the dressing room.

SUMMER.

1..2..3...

...Somewhere over the rainbow skies are blue... & the dreams that you dare to dream really do come true....

"Hello sunshine!" She hears someone say before they bump into her and wake her up.

"Oh, sorry!" Says the stranger.

"No problem," she answers still half asleep. For a moment his voice had been so clear, she could still hear the melody lingering on beyond the words. She opens her eyes to the deep blue of the cap that had been her cozy nap helper. The edge allows her a glimpse of the seat in front of her. She looks up. She had forgotten she was on a plane. She looks around. The plane was now full yet they were still on the ground. That someone had come to wake up the passenger in front of her. He didn't seem too pleased to be woken up either.

"I know you like your dreams," says one guy to the other, "but we have to move."

She smiles. *I know the feeling,* she thinks as pulls down her cap from the brim and turns to fall asleep again... *perhaps I can pick up where I left off...* Next thing she knows, she is landing. She looks out the window, it is a sunny day out. The stewardess

1...2...3...

makes the announcement that it is now safe to turn on your phones and as she does her phone starts dancing to a buzzing rhythm. Once her phone has caught up she looks at the girls group chat and sees 48 missed messages. She texts them a single word "Landed" and a smiling emoji, then looks over at her notifications. There are a couple of emails she will get to once she is at the hotel and an old notification from her IM-LISTENING account. She opens it to see it was @willandheart's post for Minnie Riperton's "Lovin' You." She looks for her music and posts Fleetwood Mac's "Don't Stop" to her stream, just then @willandheart tags her with Annie's "Tomorrow" and she laughs.

Shortly after getting off the plane she notices a little shop with tiny fluffy goats displayed right at the entrance and thinks of P. While she is buying P her gotie she gets a text from B — a catch up is most necessary, and they are both in agreement. As she heads over to baggage claim the speakers call out for a Mr. Heart to retrieve an item from special baggage desk.

"Mr. Heart, would you please come to special baggage desk to retrieve your bag."

Huh…that's a nice name… she thinks…

The message rings again: *"Mr. Heart, Mr. W. Heart."*

W. Heart? She looks down at her phone, the words @willandheart pop-out from the uncleared notification messages. *Could it be?* She turns to look for signs for the special baggage desk. It is in the same direction she is heading.

"Mr. Heart, as a token of our appreciation we would like to help you retrieve what you left behind."

She rushing over to the special baggage desk when the message coming out of the speakers suddenly stops. She stops too and turns to look at the door closest to the special baggage desk. Perhaps she will recognize the person amongst the throng of people exiting the building. Nothing. Her phone vibrates, it's a message from S: "Welcome! We are out here waiting for you!"

She goes to the band that has her bag, picks it up, and heads out to meet her friend.

S was staging a production inspired by "Twelfth Night" at a theater festival with her all-female company called "The Food Of Love." G had promised to arrive early and lend a hand with tech rehearsals. The past few months had been a whirlwind. Between the book and the exhibits she was looking forward to a little time off and hopefully a lot of dreams. It works out perfectly when S suggests they take the afternoon to relax and hang out before heading to rehearsals.

With the weather what it was, they head over to the park, where after making a stop at the ice cream truck, sit down to catch up and enjoy the sunlight. The last time she had ice cream it had been in a dream. It was a delicious ice cream sundae with honey drizzle and chocolate-flavored rainbow colored sprinkles, and because in dreams you didn't have to choose between flavor or fun — you could have both — when the lady at the counter asked if she wanted sprinkles on her ice-cream she had actually asked "Do you have chocolate flavored but rainbow colored sprinkles?"

To which the lady responded with a polite request to clarify, "I'm sorry, did you say you want chocolate or rainbow sprinkles on your ice cream?"

"Both," she ended up saying, and so her ice cream was covered in chocolate and rainbow covered sprinkles... *I have to come up with a way to actually have the option of chocolate flavored rainbow color sprinkles...* she thought... She takes her spoon and fills it with honey before dipping it into her cup and mixing everything together.

"You know, I've seen you do that a couple of times now and I've been meaning to ask. Why don't you just drizzle your ice-cream in honey?" Asks S.

"Oh, because this way the spoon stays dipped in honey and it sticks to all the ice cream spoonfuls. There's more honey flavor that way," she says.

"Huh, I'll have to try that sometime," says S, "So, how's your new book coming along?"

"Very well actually. I just finished the last of my research on Vermeer, so I was hoping to use some of my free time here to put everything together," she says.

"That's exciting," says S, "you will for sure have time for that. Tech is not going to be as bad as it sounds, you'll see. Most of the show is staged to be listened to, the visuals are largely placeholders and action queues. Be prepared for A LOT of music."

"I love the sound of it already! Pun intended." She says with a grin. "I'm here for whatever you need. How are things going with you? Are you ready for your big premiere?" she asks.

"Not at all, but I think the company is fantastic. You'll see for yourself," says S excited.

"Uff I can't wait!"

"Speaking of premieres, how was D's?"

"Fantastic. D was brilliant, I know I sound totally biased, but D does have a very natural comedic streak."

"Ah! I can't wait to see it! I've been following the buzz and it looks like it may get picked up by some big names."

"I know! It's very exciting," she says, "I hope it does. So walk me through my tomorrow, what time do you want me where for what?"

"Ok, so I was thinking we wake up around 7-7ish, get some light breakfast together and walk over to the locale. I am thinking we'll be done with Acts 1-2 around noon and then 3-4 after five. Then we'd go over all the notes, re-do the set up for Act 1, have dinner, and start all over again the next day."

"Alright. Maybe we can do breakfast to go? I'm not sure I can eat breakfast that early."

"Yeah, that sounds perfect."

"Great. So what is our bagel equivalent here? If not I can ask for a pear and a croissant from in-room dining."

"Knowing you you'd have their soup for breakfast!"

"Soup is a heartwarming all day thing thank you very much. Why what's their soup like?"

"Well I am sure they have more than one kind, but their Cullen skunk is delicious and I am sure you are going to l-ove it!"

"Sounds stinky..."

"It's creamy and cheesy and fishy... and that is not an apt description but it just fits," says S

"Oooo, then I am sure I will love it."

"Once things settle down maybe we can go for a round of golf, and then grab a bowl of soup after. I know a great little place in St. Andrews for it."

"Sign me up for that!"

" So... any updates on your er— dream-tuation?" Asks S

"On my dreamy man? I am letting the music play on," she says, "and on and on..."

"Hey music reaches where words alone sometimes cannot," says S.

"Exactly," she answers.

Dum da di di di di ... She looks around. The cafe speakers are playing the song.

"Speaking of music," she says.

"Well that song does seem to follow you around," says S laughing, "I don't think I hear it as much unless I am with you."

"It is music to my ears you know."

S just laughs and shakes her head.

She closes her eyes and takes a slow deep breath, feeling the melody's embrace as she does, "it is just such a pleasing sound," she says.

"It definitely reaches you," says S.

"That it does," She smiles, grabs her phone and posts the song to her IM-LISTENING stream alongside The Beatles' "All You Need Is Love ". @willandheart quickly likes them both, ...*huh...* she thinks... *maybe it was him...*

"I saw that smile..." Asks S curious.

She sighs, "Oh, no—this is a friend."

"A friend?" Questions S.

"Yeah, we exchange songs, it's fun."

"Oh, that friend!"

"It's funny the whole thing feels so familiar, I've never met the person. I guess when you vibe with someone there is always that feeling of familiarity."

"That's so true," says S.

G puts her phone away and dips her spoon in honey and onto her ice-cream again, her smile widens as she dances to the tune.

S looks at her friend and shakes her head, "So tell me what would you do if you saw him right now?"

"Oh, I would run to him as fast as my feet can take me," she answers immediately.

"You would just dash towards him?"

"Dash, run, fly... Wild horses wouldn't stop me! In fact if they were around I would ride one of them just to get to him faster & ask it to sprout wings," she says.

"And then what?" Asks S holding back a friendly laugh.

"And then..." she thinks back to their first encounter, "and then I'd say 'Hello', "

"Just 'hello'? You would come up to a stranger on a horse — a pegasus even—and just say 'hello'? " Says S.

"Well, a) there is a very high probability that he is not a stranger — emphasis on probability — , and b) 'hello' is always a good start," she says.

"I guess 'hello' is always a good start," reiterates S.

A long table runs along the stage with platters and platters of fruit overflowing from every corner. There were pears and oranges, grapes and grapefruits, lemons and apples, mangoes and peaches, kiwis and cherries, and then sunflowers and orchids blooming from the spaces in between.

The table had chairs, on the back and front, the side chairs were placed sporadically along the stage for character interactions. S had characters interacting with the food and the chairs, and as they moved a different instrument sounded. There was a trumpet, a piano (steinway in birch sitting comfortably on the far right corner of the stage), a mandolin, a violin, a drum, a banjo, a guitar, a tambourine, a pair of maracas, a marimba, a bass, and a cello.

The play starts with Duke Orsino's elemental line "If music be the food of love play on," and then it unravels during the course of a feast. The basis of it being that only essential moments of dialogue are used and where dialogue is not found visual movements are intertwined with the sounds that represent each character to support the narrative as key melodies express the character's transformation throughout the story. It was a beautiful love story expressed in melody and set to sound.

By the time Act 2 was done, a cluster of jumbled mini events had led the sound system to utter silence and repairs were needed in order to continue. The entirety of the show was based on music inspiring love, which meant music was the foundation for the show, and music without sound — well — it just was more silence than intended. It would take about 2 hours to set up the new system and as everyone breaks to catch-up later in the afternoon she decides to go for a walk and perhaps find a good donut shop to bring everyone a little sweetness for the rest of rehearsals.

As she texts S that she will catch up with her later, she receives a notification from IM-LISTENING of @willandheart's latest post, Neil Diamond's "Sweet Caroline," she likes the post and replies with Brandie Carlisle's "Heaven Is A Place On Earth," and she keeps walking.

She sighs, it had been a few months since she had sent her reply... Her book was doing well enough that it could be easily found... She just hoped she wasn't too late... She did tend to be late... *What if she was late?... Would it change anything? No, not for her,* she thought. No matter the distance, no matter the time, she was still going to love him, *always was simply a given with him,* she knew that. It was a funny thought to think she used to be scared of opening hear heart. It didn't feel like it had had any trouble opening to him, it was immediate, simply a recognition of something that already was.

No matter what happened next she would always love him, and she would always be grateful for every precious moment that brought wonder and love back into her life... she would always be grateful for him... Whenever they met, whenever he appeared in her waking life — and she was sure now that it would happen — it would be perfect.

This time, she would be ready from the start. If there is something this experience had taught her is that you have to believe happy endings exist, if not you could just walk past them and not recognize them. *You can't plan the perfect moment*, she remembered, *you can, however, let it happen...*

As she continues her walk, her thoughts steady in this train, she sees a violinist set up her gear to start playing on the street, she looks up, the name of the street "Hope St" catches her attention. *Hope* she thinks, *hope is everything.* A tabby cat crosses the street in front of her just as the pub on the corner is taking out a crate with old glass bottles. She is not sure but she can almost see the cat drinking the spillage of milk that is running out of one of the crates and ever so slightly down the road. Just then the violinist starts playing Tchaikovsky's Sleeping Beauty's "Once Upon A Dream," the sound catches her attention and she laughs at the serendipity of the moment. She opens her phone, takes a short video to remind herself to stay hopeful, then finds the Disney version of the song in her music and posts it to her IM-LISTENING stream. *What are the odds?* She thinks.

Odds... everything seemed to be pairing up rather... She is walking with this in mind when she stumbles upon a clearing. Something is familiar about it. The last time she found herself in open green fields such as these it had been the day they met. She had gone to a music festival, at least in her dreams she had, and it had been one of the happiest moments of her life. She takes a slight right turn to explore it. It takes a second for her to recognize the green space before her. She feels something on her shoulder. It is just a friendly ladybug that stopped by for a quick hello.

She sighs, she is the only one there. Her phone vibrates in her pocket. She looks down @willandheart has liked her post. She smiles. She looks up, long fields of green fill her heart with hope. Perfect natural harmony abounds all around her, she closes her eyes and takes a long deep breath. She can hear steady footsteps on the grass reaching the surrounding area... someone approaches... *or maybe it's a deer...* she thinks.

"Excuse me, could you help me? I am trying to find my way back to—"

She knows that voice. She opens her eyes. She *knows* that voice. As she turns she knows, she knows she will find *him* standing right in front of *her*. She turns. A single word is uttered in blissful simultaneity:

" ...YOU... "

His earphone falls onto his hoodie. The song playing rings softly in the background... the instruments lead a waltz and the lyrics make themselves known *"...I know you I walked with you Once Upon A Dream..."*

The End & The Beginning

1...2...3...

...1...2...3...4...

P.S. For those curious, the latest IM-LISTENING post
is 2 Cody Johnson "The Painter..."

A Note From The Author:

Hi, my name is Isabel and I love to write. Writing is my favorite window into possibility! Through it I discover windows from which others experience the world around us, and with it I get to express what I see from my own window into the world. I hope you always leave your window to possibility open and find the wonders that await you on the other side!

1..2..3...